Happy reading
Zara Osborne

NS Buchman

The Secret Dinosaur
Giants Awake!
and
Hunters Attack

N.S. Blackman

Dinosaur Books

Text and illustrations copyright © 2014, 2017
N.S. Blackman

All Rights Reserved
Published by Dinosaur Books Ltd, London
This edition: 2017
www.dinosaurbooks.co.uk
Dinoteks™ Sonya McGilchrist

ISBN 978-0-9930105-9-0
British Library Cataloguing in Publication Data
A CIP catalogue record for this book is available from
the British Library

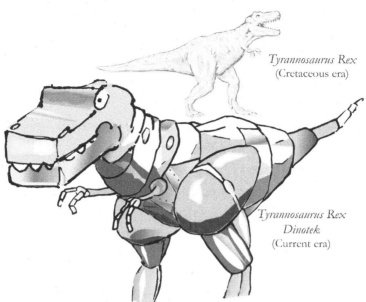

Tyrannosaurus Rex
(Cretaceous era)

*Tyrannosaurus Rex
Dinotek*
(Current era)

The Secret Dinosaur
Giants Awake!

Centrosaurus
(Cretaceous era)

Centrosaurus Dinotek
(Current era)

Also available in the **Dinotek Adventures** series:

The Secret Dinosaur: Jurassic Adventure
The Secret Dinosaur: Night Rescue
The Secret Dinosaur: The Silver Giant
The Secret Dinosaur: The Sky Raptor

The Lost Dinosaur (for younger readers)

Search for The Dinotek Adventures
or find out more at
www.dinoteks.com

The very beginning
. . . .

One Rainy Night

Marlin Maxton knew that all dinosaurs were extinct. He was sure of it. Of course there were still birds – there were plenty of those – but the big dinosaurs, the really big ones, they were gone and nothing like them would ever be seen again.

That's what Marlin thought, right up until the night he visited his uncle's workshop.

It was getting late, almost dark, and rain was drumming on the workshop roof. Marlin was perched on the sofa, sipping hot chocolate and enjoying the cosy feeling as the wind rattled and whistled around outside.

Uncle Gus was always making things – fixing things together and coming up with strange inventions. Some people thought he was foolish – and it's true he was a bit scruffy and more than a bit forgetful – but Marlin knew he was really very clever.

On this particular night Uncle Gus had the parts from a very old engine laid out on the floor, waiting to be repaired. He was sitting completely still, thinking about something (something complicated, probably) when suddenly he looked up.

"School trip to the museum tomorrow, Marlin?" he said. "I wonder if you'll see old Protos?"

He took a sip of his drink and his eyes twinkled at Marlin through the rising steam.

"Protos? Who's that?"

"Who's that?" he laughed. "Did I never tell you?"

Marlin shook his head.

"No."

"That's odd…" frowned Uncle Gus – and he leaned forward. "Never mind, I'll tell you now. Years ago, when I was young,

I thought Protos was the best thing in the museum. He's a metal dinosaur."

A gust of wind rattled the workshop windows and Marlin snuggled into his fleece. He listened as his uncle described the creature.

"Life-size he was – very big – a

Centrosaurus. Four legs, thick as tree trunks and a long curving horn right on the front of his nose."

He stretched out his arms, as wide as they would go, to show how long the horn was.

"I remember he used to stand all by himself in his own special room at the back of the dinosaur gallery."

Marlin was eager to hear more but Uncle Gus was now standing up and working on the engine again.

"But what's so special about him?"

"Eh? Who?"

"Protos!"

Uncle Gus put down his spanner and smiled.

"Well, maybe you'll find out tomorrow. If you see him. But I don't suppose you will. It was all so long ago he's probably not even there now…"

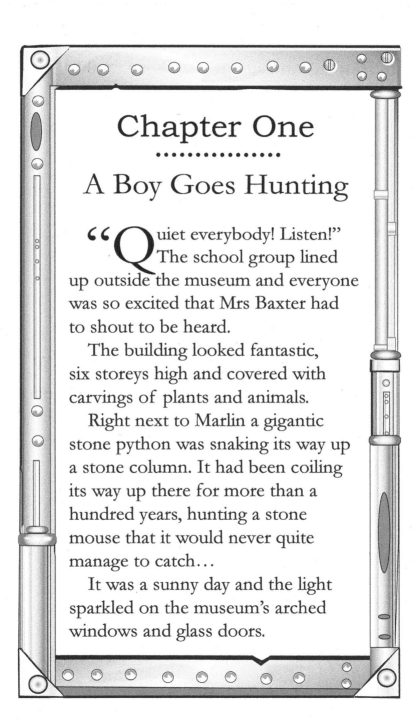

Chapter One

·················

A Boy Goes Hunting

"**Q**uiet everybody! Listen!"
The school group lined up outside the museum and everyone was so excited that Mrs Baxter had to shout to be heard.

The building looked fantastic, six storeys high and covered with carvings of plants and animals.

Right next to Marlin a gigantic stone python was snaking its way up a stone column. It had been coiling its way up there for more than a hundred years, hunting a stone mouse that it would never quite manage to catch...

It was a sunny day and the light sparkled on the museum's arched windows and glass doors.

But unfortunately it also shone on the bald and frowning head of a man in a suit. He was waiting for them at the entrance.

Mr Oliver Grubbler scowled. He did

not like working at the museum. He didn't like the building, or the wonderful things inside it, or the people who came to look at them.

There was just one thing about his job that he did enjoy and that was handing out worksheets. He gave worksheets to every school group that visited.

The whole class groaned when they saw

his bulging pile of papers and that made

Grubbler a little bit happier.

As the children filed through the door, one by one, he handed the sheets out.

"No running, no shouting, no touching anything," he growled. Then he added: "You can look at things, but not for too long."

Marlin's heart sank. With all this work there would be no time to hunt for dinosaurs.

******

Marlin rushed to fill in his sheet. There were pages of questions about animals and plants and they seemed to go on forever. But Marlin worked fast and finished in record time. He stuffed

his pencil into his bag and looked up. His friends were still writing.

"Maybe I could explore for a few minutes..." Marlin thought to himself. "I won't be long..."

That's what he thought.

******

The dinosaur gallery was amazing. Marlin leaned back and stared up at the huge fossil skeletons towering above him. There was a Diplodocus and a Brachiosaurus

Cerotopsi

Spino

(even taller) and straight ahead loomed a
Stegosaurus, its back lined with jagged-
plates. The bones hung on almost-invisible
wires and seemed to float in the air.

Spinosaurus

Even better were the life-size
models. A group
of raptors was
picking over
the carcass
of a dead
herbivore –
and creeping

up behind, a fully grown Allosaurus was about to spring on them in a classic ambush attack.

But Marlin searched everywhere and there was no sign of Uncle Gus's special Centrosaurus.

Disappointed, he turned to leave. And as he did, he noticed the doorway. There was another room, right at the back of the gallery, almost hidden behind a display of fossils. He moved closer. Maybe this was the place...

Somewhere far off a clock struck twelve. Marlin was starting to feel hungry, it would soon be time to go back to his class, but he *had* to find out what was through that doorway.

He crept forwards and peered into the shadows.

Chapter Two

· · · · · · · · · · · · · · · ·

The Forgotten Giant

Some people looking into that room would just have walked away again. They would have decided there was nothing special about Protos because he wasn't very realistic, not compared with the big models in the main hall. Instead of having life-like, plastic skin he was made completely out of metal: sheets of armour-plate hammered together, bronze and silver, shining softly in the dim light.

Some people would have walked away – but not Marlin.

Marlin could see it straight away. He could see that Protos really was amazing. The soft metal glow of his armour made him seem *more* alive, not less.

Marlin crept forward into the room. He wanted to look closer.

He *had* to look closer!

The creature was built so beautifully. Some of his pieces were riveted together, while others were carefully welded, or held with bolts. Marlin spotted a sign on the wall but when he went over to look he found that it was covered in dust.

Doesn't anyone clean in this room?
It was as if the place had been forgotten.
He reached out
and wiped away
the grime with
his sleeve.
"Model
Centrosaurus…"
Marlin repeated.

But he knew
the sign wasn't
quite right.

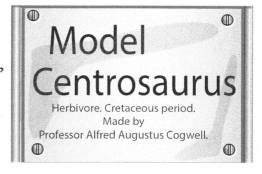

Model Centrosaurus

Herbivore. Cretaceous period.
Made by
Professor Alfred Augustus Cogwell.

Protos definitely wasn't just a model,
he was a machine. Marlin was certain of
it. There were wheels and gears and wires
around the creature's back legs and some
other parts that had come loose over the
years.

He leaned forward to look at the broken
bits. He didn't think about what he was
doing, and he didn't remember what Mr
Grubbler had said about not touching
things. He was so used to doing repairs
in Uncle Gus's garage that he just started

17

working. He twisted two wires together (making connections) and popped a pin back into place (joining things up). He flicked a switch, and nodded to himself.

"That should do it..."

"I think so," a voice replied. "And if you wouldn't mind screwing the cover back on it helps keep out the dust."

Marlin jumped backwards. He'd been caught!

He stood, his heart racing, and prepared to face the angry museum manager. But instead he found himself looking into the shining glass eye of the dinosaur.

The creature had come to life.

******

The air all around Protos fizzed and crackled with energy – golden sparks flew, as if somebody had set off a firework.

The creature shook himself.

"Ahh! That's better!" Then he blinked.

"Is it just you?" he asked. "No-one else?"

He looked around the room. His deep voice sounded disappointed.

"Strange. They told me to expect a few more.

Fizzz!

Well never mind, the main thing is that you're here. Now! Shall we begin?"

"B...begin?" stuttered Marlin.

"Of course, time is precious, you should never sit around or you might as well be a fossil!"

The machine creature cleared his throat.

"Ahem! Ladies and gentlemen, girls and boys welcome to the Dinoteks Exhibition, the Greatest Show on Earth! My name is Protos and I will be your guide..."

The creature took a heavy, lumbering step

forward – THUD! – and Marlin jumped back out of the way.

"Thank you. Now, if you'll kindly follow me…"

Protos moved surprisingly quickly for his size. One of his back legs seemed to drag a bit – and his foot scraped the ground – but he heaved himself forwards happily enough and didn't seem to notice.

"…imagine travelling back through time to the world of the dinosaurs. Close your eyes and think of it. A hundred million years ago – it sounds like a long age but in the life of the Earth that's just the blink of an eye – and in those days our planet was a very different place: a place of wonder, a place of beauty, a place of danger…"

Suddenly Protos stopped, and looked straight at Marlin.

"Speaking of danger," he said, lowering his voice. "Please don't be frightened. The creatures you are about to see are all perfectly safe. I especially want you to remember this when you see Flame, our T-Rex. He may look fierce but he's only acting. Also, don't

THUD!

stand too close to Steg when he turns round, his tail is sharp and no matter how often I remind him he forgets."

He continued out through the door – then stopped again.

"Ah. One other thing. We have a Pterosaur. He's very sweet but if he offers to take you flying, just say no – he can't actually fly you see, he just thinks he can. Got that? Good – this way!"

And Protos was off again.

"Where was I? Ah yes…a place of wonder, a place of beauty, a place of danger. Thanks to the miracle of modern technology, you will see this ancient world brought back to life again. The Dinoteks combine the very latest in intelligent software and sophisticated mechanics…"

CLUNK!

Suddenly a large piece of metal dropped off of Protos's tail and rolled across the floor. He continued walking and didn't seem to notice, so Marlin picked it up for him and quickly pushed it back into place.

"…in fact, Ladies and Gentlemen, the Dinoteks are living, thinking creatures, just like you…"

Protos paused and looked over his shoulder.

"Actually, I won't bother with all that 'Ladies and Gentlemen' stuff if you don't mind. It seems a bit silly as there's only one of you. What *is* your name?"

"Marlin."

"Marlin! That's better. Now, follow me Marlin and try to keep up…"

Protos lumbered right across the dinosaur gallery and to Marlin's surprise didn't stop there. He went out through a door and into a long, narrow passage.

"Er, shouldn't we be back in the dinosaur gallery?" Marlin asked.

"In that old place? No, no – the Dinoteks Show is much better than that! Come along now, this way…"

The corridor they were now in looked much older than the rest of the museum and Marlin noticed that the floor was covered in dust, just like the sign on the wall in Protos' room. The passage was poorly lit, and in several places cobwebs dangled from the ceiling.

"...now prepare to be amazed. As we step through these doors, you will think you have journeyed back through time!"

There were double doors right in front of them, twice as big as ordinary doors. Protos stopped and looked at Marlin. His eyes were sparkling with excitement.

"Ready Marlin?"

"Er, ready – I think..."

"Then follow me!"

He lowered his great armoured head and shoved against the doors. The hinges strained for a moment then gave a loud, rusty crack and swung open.

"Welcome to the greatest show on earth!" Protos announced.

And in they both went.

Chapter Three

The Lost Room

The room was a mess. It was dark. Piles of junk were heaped up everywhere and a thick layer of dust covered the floor. Protos looked around confused.

"Flame! Steg! Are you ready?"

But there was no reply.

"Dacky? Come on everybody. Our first visitor is here. We need to start the show…"

His voice trailed off. It echoed into silence. The old creature stood there looking around him and in that moment Marlin felt very sorry for him.

"I don't understand…"

Marlin came to stand next to him.

"I think something went wrong," he said gently. "How long did you say you've been waiting for your show to begin?"

"How long? Let me see…it was Friday afternoon…the Professor said everything was nearly finished and…" Protos frowned, confused. "I waited…then I took a quick nap and then…then you woke me up."

The creature looked at him.

"It can't have been *very* long… can it?"

Marlin went back to the door and fumbled around for a light switch. He flicked it on – to reveal an amazing collection of metal dinosaurs, all around the room. But they were all covered in dust, from head to toe. It had settled on them layer by layer, year by year, burying them like fossils.

"I…I remember now…" Protos said quietly. "I waited, but the Professor didn't come … I kept waiting…I kept looking out for him…but then I fell asleep…"

He looked at Marlin.

"That's it, isn't it? I've been asleep for years."

And a great, oily tear rolled down his metal face.

Marlin sat with the old Centrosaurus for a long time in the lost room. The creature shuffled around trying to tidy things up, and Marlin helped him. But it was no use, there was too much mess.

Then, far off, he heard a bell and suddenly he remembered his class – he had

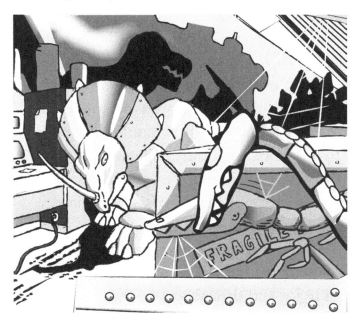

to get back. He would be in trouble!

"Yes, you must go at once," said Protos. "I've kept you talking too long. Come on…"

And he heaved himself round and cleared his throat.

"Ladies and Gentlemen – I mean Marlin – thank you for coming to the Greatest Show on Earth. I am sorry that due to technical difficulties the Dinoteks were not able to continue with today's show. I do hope this didn't spoil your visit to the museum too much…"

His back leg was dragging as he headed for the door.

"Wait!" cried Marlin, running after him. "My visit to the museum wasn't spoiled and I don't care that the show couldn't happen!"

Protos looked at him and smiled.

"Thank you Marlin. I'm glad it was you who came to our first show. It was nice meeting you and – "

Then suddenly there was a loud BANG and a wisp of smoke curled around Protos's leg. He looked down.

"Oh dear," he whispered. "I think that was my battery…can't stay awake…"

He looked up and smiled.

"Thank you for coming Ladies and Gentlemen…I mean Marlin…"

And that was the last word he said. His head nodded, his eyes closed.

"Wait!" exclaimed Marlin. "Don't sleep! Tell me how to help you!"

But Protos didn't reply. He stood there like all his friends, no longer alive but just a statue.

******

Marlin sprinted down the old corridor and back through the dinosaur gallery to find his class. His mind was racing. He had to find a way to help Protos. He couldn't just leave him standing there, forever forgotten…

He was so busy trying to think of what to do that he didn't notice Oliver Grubbler step out in front of him and he went smack into the big man's stomach.

"Whoa! Where do you think you're going boy?!"

"I...I got lost!" exclaimed Marlin. "I'm looking for my class!"

Grubbler rubbed his stomach and glared at him suspiciously.

"It's that way," he grunted, jabbing his finger towards the exit. "And no running!"

Relieved, Marlin walked away as quickly as he dared. Grubbler called after him.

"I've got my eye on you!"

Chapter Four

· · · · · · · · · · · · · · · ·

The Thing That
All Machines Hate

Marlin tried to tell his teacher what had happened, but she was too busy to listen.

"Line up with the others now, or we'll be late!" she said firmly.

When he got home his mum and dad were too busy to listen too. They were loading boxes into their car, getting ready for another business trip. His mum smiled as she hurried past.

Marlin realised there was only one person who would listen: Uncle Gus. The quickest way to his workshop was down the garden, over the fence and along an alleyway.

Marlin sprinted all the way.

The workshop was a little brick building, covered in ivy, with a patched-up roof of rusty metal. It nestled in the shadow of an oak tree and a rope had been looped over one of the branches, with a tyre for Marlin to swing on.

A friendly orange light was peeping out through the workshop's open door.

A few minutes later Uncle Gus listened in silence as Marlin told his story. He looked thoughtful and nodded from time to time. His bushy eyebrows were set in a deep frown.

Marlin had never seen him look quite so serious.

"You're sure? The old dinosaur really came to life lad?"

Marlin nodded.

"And he spoke to you?"

"Yes!"

Then Uncle Gus chuckled.

"Well that's very odd. Very odd indeed. I've been talking to my car for years but she never answers me!"

He hurried across the workshop to a shelf piled with junk.

"Where is it, where is it now? ...Aha!"

He turned round smiling and handed Marlin an old cloth bag.

"The question is," he said "what are you going to do about these Dinoteks now?"

"I really want to help them," Marlin answered. "But I don't know how!"

"Then what you need is a *plan*."

He rubbed his hands together happily and stood thinking. Uncle Gus liked making plans, and they were usually very good ones. Marlin waited hopefully.

Uncle Gus spoke at last.

"I can't tell you exactly what to do," he said. "But I can tell you where to start. Do

you remember last year when we took
that old steam engine apart? We cleaned
all the pieces, made some repairs, then put
everything back together?"

Marlin nodded.

"Do you remember – what is the one
thing that all machines hate?" asked Uncle
Gus.

Marlin thought about it.

"Dirt?"

"That's right lad – brilliant boy! Dirt and
dust! It gets right into them, see? And stops
them working."

Now Uncle Gus nodded at the cloth bag
that he'd given Marlin. Marlin looked inside:
there was a pile of rags, three jars of metal
cleaner and a big can of machine oil.

******

Cleaning the Dinoteks was a big job and
Marlin went back to the museum every
evening for two weeks.

He went straight after school and crept
through the galleries to the hidden passage.
He made sure nobody was looking –

especially the horrible Mr Grubbler – then
pushed hard on the big double doors. They
creaked at first and did not want to move
but then a gap opened for him to squeeze
through.

Each day he had with him his cleaning
bag and his lunchbox so he wouldn't get
hungry.

Each day he went home again at six
o'clock.

"Working late today?" his mum would say.

Marlin always answered yes (which was true) and she never actually asked what he was working on.

"Keep it up," his dad would say, patting him on the back.

******

Now something strange happened. Marlin discovered that cleaning could be fun.

Of course he never liked tidying up at home, but here in the secret room he was happy to wipe off grime, scrape out dirt, wash, brush and polish. It was exciting.

He cleaned the Dinoteks one by one and he dripped machine oil into their joints. He started with the two little ones (the Troodons), then the Pterosaur and then he went on to the giants.

When he got to the Stegosaurus he needed a ladder to reach its armoured back-plates.

Finally he worked on Protos and then the T-Rex, which towered over all of them.

Marlin tried to remember what Protos had called the Rex...*Flame, wasn't it? Flame, yes that was it.*

"Time to wake up Flame..." Marlin said softly as he cleaned.

******

Day by day the dinosaurs looked less like old fossils. Their metal skins began to glow.

They were coming back to life.

Chapter Five

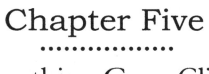

Something Goes Click!

Now the secret room wasn't gloomy any more. Now it really was magical, just as Protos had promised. Everything was glowing, even the metal trees with their hanging branches danced and shimmered with life.

Just one thing spoiled it.

The Dinoteks stayed frozen.

Marlin had worked hard. He had cleaned the creatures from top to bottom. He had done everything Uncle Gus had told him, but it seemed to make no difference.

All the time Marlin kept hoping to hear a friendly voice suddenly boom out and see those sparkling lights like little fireworks again.

But it didn't happen.

"There must be something else," he said to himself. "Something I need to do. Something I haven't thought of…"

And he was saying these exact words — "something I haven't thought of" — when it happened.

There was a click.

Yes — he was wiping his polishing cloth over the Protos's front leg and *something clicked.*

A metal plate moved under his hand and then popped open on a hinge! Marlin leaned forward to look. There was a space full of wires. And in the middle of that space was a grey cylinder. It had silver tips at each end.

Marlin reached in. The cylinder was smooth and cold.

"It looks like…like a huge battery…"

He gave the cylinder a tug and it came loose in his hand. It was very heavy.

A battery…

What if all the Dinoteks have them?

He ran over to the Stegosaurus and pressed his leg in the same way — a hatch popped open. There was another space exactly the same, a tangle of wires and a long grey cylinder.

And when he searched each one of the other creatures he found the same thing.

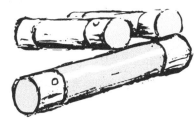

This has to be the answer!

Quickly, he pulled out all the cylinders and tucked them into his bag. Then he heaved it over his shoulder. It was really heavy but he knew what he had to do.

He would carry the cylinders to Uncle Gus.

******

"You're right!" beamed his uncle. "I haven't seen batteries like this for years – in fact I can't remember when I last did."

He was holding one up to the light, peering at it.

"What a lucky find – magnificent! One of these would give your creatures all the power they need – if it was fully charged…"

He shoved the battery back into Marlin's hand and began searching for something at the back of the workshop. A moment later he was dragging a wooden crate out from under a workbench.

Marlin rushed to help.

"That's right lad, let's get it into the light…"

At last, when the crate was out in the open, Marlin could see that it was very old and heaped full of junk, tools and strange bits of machinery.

Uncle Gus began rummaging through it, pulling things out.

"Let me see now …I'm sure I put it in here…AHA!"

He stood up triumphantly, clutching a golden box. It had two handles, one on each side, two clips hanging from it on wires and a little dial on the front like a clock-face.

"It's a universal power-charger," he

explained. "It's a very clever tool. I invented it myself — I can't quite remember why, but I'm sure it must have been for something important..."

He picked up the cylinder battery again and attached the clips to it, one to each silver tip.

At first nothing happened. Uncle Gus peered intently at the clock face.

"Come on now...don't let me down..."

Then suddenly the needle twitched and began to move around the dial.

"Aha! That's more like it!"

Uncle Gus beamed and gave the golden machine a gentle pat.

"It's powering up Marlin. What did I tell you? This little beauty will bring anything back to life."

Marlin grinned. "How long will it take?"

"Oh, not long lad, not long. Come back in the morning. By then I'll have all your batteries working perfectly."

****

That night Marlin had a fantastic dream. In it, he arrived at the museum to find Protos standing at the door waiting for him, his polished skin glowing brightly.

"Welcome to the Great Dinotek Show!" exclaimed the dream creature. "Everybody's waiting for you inside. Except for Dacky. Look up there! I admit I'm a bit surprised, but guess what? He can fly after all!"

Marlin looked up and saw the Pterosaur swooping round far, far above the museum. As the creature crossed the sky the sun glinted on his golden head-crest.

He was clutching a banner in his claws.

'Dinoteks Show Now Open!' said the writing on the banner. 'All Welcome!"

"Wait here!" exclaimed Marlin. "I'm going to get all my friends!"

And in his dream, with his heart racing, he rushed off to school to tell the whole class.

And that's when he woke up.

That happy dream lingered in his mind and he lay in bed smiling. Then he remembered why it was he felt so excited.

Today, the batteries would be ready.
Today it would really happen.

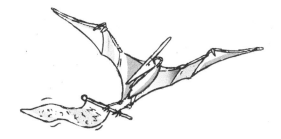

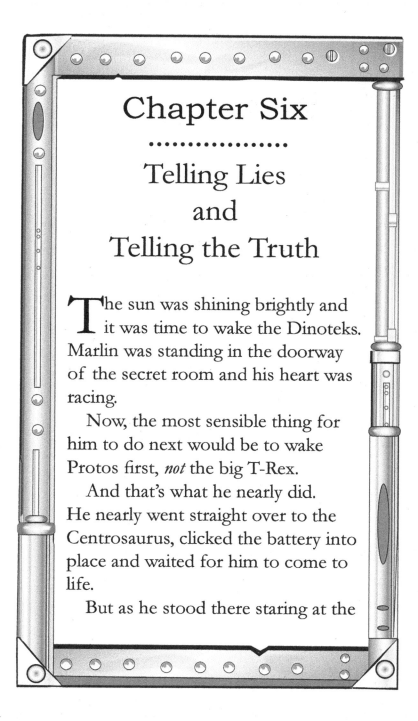

Chapter Six

....

Telling Lies
and
Telling the Truth

The sun was shining brightly and it was time to wake the Dinoteks. Marlin was standing in the doorway of the secret room and his heart was racing.

Now, the most sensible thing for him to do next would be to wake Protos first, *not* the big T-Rex.

And that's what he nearly did. He nearly went straight over to the Centrosaurus, clicked the battery into place and waited for him to come to life.

But as he stood there staring at the

Dinoteks, it was the T-Rex that he was really looking at. In fact he couldn't take his eyes off it. Maybe it was because the towering creature had taken so long to clean. Or maybe he thought it would be nice for Protos to wake up and find one of his friends already awake and waiting for him.

Maybe.

Or perhaps it was something else. There was something about the golden-headed predator that drew Marlin forwards and made him want to plug the battery in. He wanted to do it even though his hands were trembling just a bit.

He stepped up to the huge clawed foot.

"OK," he whispered. "I'll just see what happens if…"

And that's as far as he got. Because a meaty hand clapped down on his shoulder.

"Caught you at last!" growled Mr Grubbler.

Marlin jumped up – but the museum manager held him tight.

******

Marlin sat miserably in Oliver Grubbler's office. He was alone and the door was locked.

After ordering him to sit down Grubbler had stomped off without a word. His footsteps had faded and then the room plunged into silence.

Now Marlin sat alone and it was so quiet he felt his heart beating. He wished he had a phone to call Uncle Gus.

He waited and it felt as if he was waiting forever, until at last the heavy footsteps returned. For an instant Marlin wondered whether he should hide under the desk but it was too late. A key stabbed and rattled in the lock and the door swung open.

"I've got him trapped in here, Inspector..."

Grubbler stepped in and pointed at him.

"Here he is. This is the thief!"

A woman leaned in behind him and peered at Marlin. She had grey hair and dark, stern eyes.

"Hmm. He doesn't look like a thief Mr Grubbler. He looks like a child."

Grubbler snorted.

"Don't be fooled! When you run a busy museum you soon learn that children and criminals are often the same thing."

The woman didn't reply to that. She came and sat on a chair next to Marlin.

"My name is Inspector Bailey," she said. "I'm a police detective."

Her eyes were very serious but her voice was kind and Marlin began to feel a little less afraid.

"Mr Grubbler says you've been creeping into the museum and stealing things. Have you?"

Marlin hesitated, unsure what to say. He knew his story would sound like it was made up. Across the room he could see Mr Grubbler staring at him.

Marlin decided to tell the truth.

"I haven't stolen anything. I've been repairing the dinosaurs. I want to bring them back to life."

Inspector Bailey's eyebrows lifted.

"Ha!" laughed Grubbler. "See? He's a liar as well as a thief!"

But the detective kept looking at Marlin.

"How could you bring dinosaurs back to life?" she asked.

Marlin took a deep breath.

"Because I'm not talking about fossils – I'm talking about machines, living machines."

Marlin took the detective and the museum manager back to the secret room. Mr Grubbler stood by the door with his arms obstinately folded while Inspector Bailey walked among the Dinoteks.

"And you say you cleaned all these machines up? All by yourself?"

"Yes."

She was staring up at the T-Rex in wonder.

"When I found them they were covered in dust. I don't think anyone even knew they were here."

He pointed to the cloth bag that was still on the floor where he'd left it.

"I was about to put their batteries in and wake them up."

"That's a lie!" exclaimed Grubbler. "And anyway, this room has always been perfectly clean. There's never any mess in my museum!"

Inspector Bailey thought about this. She had noticed there was a lot of grime on the floor in the corridor leading to this room. And she had also spotted some very strange footprints there. They were very large

footprints.
Of course
the boy's story
about waking up dinosaurs was silly, but...
She looked thoughtfully at Marlin and then

leaned down to pick up one of the grey cylinders from the bag.

"Well it certainly looks like a battery," she said. "I suppose there's only one way to find out..."

She handed the cylinder to Marlin.

"Would you like to plug it in?"

Mr Grubbler gasped and backed away towards the door.

"Really Inspector!" he spluttered. "I'm not sure that's a good idea..."

But quickly, before the detective could change her mind, Marlin hurried over to the T-Rex. He pushed the battery into its leg and – CLICK! – it snapped into place.

Marlin flipped the cover shut and stepped immediately back, like somebody lighting the fuse on a dangerous firework.

Then all three of them held their breath.

Chapter Seven

....

Dinosaur Clues

Inspector Bailey's car rolled smoothly up the hill towards Marlin's house. She was giving him a ride home. He sat slumped in the passenger seat and felt miserable.

The T-Rex hadn't moved.

"Don't worry Marlin, I know you're not a thief," Inspector Bailey said. "But it's probably best if you keep away from the museum for a while. No point upsetting Mr Grubbler."

"OK," Marlin nodded.

The detective glanced at him and smiled.

"When I was your age I loved dinosaurs too. I used to wish they'd come to life."

Marlin wanted to tell her it wasn't just a wish – it was real – but instead he just nodded.

He liked her. He didn't want her to think he was a liar.

******

For once Uncle Gus wasn't in his workshop – the lights were all off and the door was locked.

Marlin's parents weren't home yet so he made himself a sandwich and sat staring gloomily out of the window.

Why hadn't it worked? Why had the T-Rex not come to life? As soon as Uncle Gus came home Marlin would ask him.

Across the road the lights came on in his friend Daniel's house. Marlin decided to go and see him instead.

Daniel was setting up a train track for his little brother Max, so Marlin joined in. When it was ready they showed Max how to use the trains to push marbles around.

It was a good game and Marlin forgot his gloomy mood. But then one of the trains began to slow down.

"Quick," said Daniel. "Let's change the battery."

And Marlin's heart sank because that reminded him again about the Dinoteks.

He sighed. It was getting dark outside anyway, and time for him to go. He said goodbye and headed back across the road.

But as he walked something strange happened. He had a very odd feeling that he was being watched. He glanced around. The road was empty.

"I'm just tired," he told himself.

And that's when he tripped over the broken paving stone.

"Ouch!

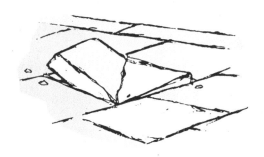

He picked himself up and looked at it. The stone was cracked clean in half and one edge was sticking up. It was as if something unusually heavy had pressed down on it.

Funny...I'm sure it wasn't like that before.

He pushed the edge down with his foot so nobody else would trip. Then he hurried on into his house.

He didn't notice that the paving stone wasn't the only thing mysteriously damaged. Just down the road a lamppost was glowing with a friendly orange light. But it was strangely bent – about half way up – as if something very large had bumped into it.

******

Marlin woke up suddenly. It was the middle of the night and there was a noise outside his window.

He sat up and blinked. He was dreaming. No! There it was again!

TAP...TAP TAP...TAP...

He slipped out of bed and crept over to the curtains. The floor was cold under his feet and the air was chilly but he hardly noticed.

He reached out with one finger and nudged a crack in the curtains.

WOOOOSH!

Something very fast flashed past – silver in the moonlight – and was gone.

Marlin jumped back, his heart racing. "What was that?!"

He edged forwards again. He pulled the curtains open wider this time and peered out.

At first he saw nothing but then he noticed the strange marks on the lawn. All over, the grass was churned up and muddy as if something heavy had been racing around on it.

Then he saw it.

A creature standing at the end of the garden.

Just under the apple tree, next to the garden gate, was a little silver dinosaur with a long whip tail and a slender neck.
It cocked its head to one side, blinked and looked right at him.

There was no mistaking it. It was one of the Troodons from the museum.

Chapter Eight

·················

Into the Night

No time to get dressed! Marlin shoved on his sweater and ran to the back door. He stuck his bare feet into his trainers.

Through the window he could still see it – the creature was still under the apple tree.

It had lowered its head and was sniffing around in the grass, poking its nose at something – a fallen apple?

Marlin opened the door – CLICK! – and its head jerked up. The Troodon stared at him with its bright, glass eyes.

Marlin took a step forward, very slowly so as not to frighten it. He held his hands gently out in front of him.

"Hello…hello there…"

The creature stood totally still.

"My name is Marlin…don't be frightened…"

He was half way across the lawn and the Troodon had still not moved.

"…what's your name?…"

Marlin edged forward again.

But before he could take another step something huge loomed over him and grabbed him from behind.

He went up.

His stomach lurched, the ground fell away and suddenly he was looking down on the world from a great height. The little creature, now far below, blinked up at him.

It turned with a flick of its tail and ran off.

Then Marlin felt himself being thrown upwards. He twisted in the air for a second before two steel jaws snapped shut around him.

******

It was dark and a cold wind rushed over him. But Marlin guessed exactly where he was.

Rows of teeth surrounded him like prison bars. He was inside the mouth of the Dinotek T-Rex.

The creature was running very fast, away from his house. Through the gaps between the teeth Marlin could see the world outside racing by, trees, buildings, lights, all flying past incredibly quickly.

But he couldn't look properly because with each thunderous step he was bounced around, like a lost boat on a stormy sea.

He reached out and grabbed one of the teeth.

"Stop!" he shouted. "Put me down!"

But the creature ignored him and raced on.

Chapter Nine

·············

Voices in the Dark

The T-Rex was slowing down. The footsteps now became a stomping walk and the wind stopped blowing.

Then Marlin heard voices. Strange voices – clucking, cawing and not-quite-human.

"It's Flame! And Siggy! They're back – open the doors!" called one.

"Inside everyone, quick, get out of sight!" came another.

The great jaws holding Marlin lowered. The teeth parted, and he was tipped sprawling onto the ground.

It was cold and dark – too dark to see a thing – and now the voices were chattering all around him.

It was the Dinoteks, Marlin was sure of it. They were all here except for Protos. His deep and gentle voice wasn't one of them.

"Is this really him? Is this the thief?" (*A sharp voice – was that the Stegosaurus?*)

"Of course it is!" (*A rumbling voice – definitely the T-Rex*). "The trail was easy to follow. I could smell him even out there."

"And I tricked him!" (*A voice so small it was almost a squeak – obviously a Troodon*). "I tricked him into coming out!"

"That's true, Siggy had a good idea there," replied the deep voice. "I wanted to bite the roof off the house but he just tapped on the window and the thief came out!"

"The thief is very small," the sharp voice said. "I thought he would be bigger."

"All humans are small," the big voice replied.

"But what's it like? Out there? On the outside?" This was a new voice. It cawed, like a crow. (*Wings? The Pterosaur?*)

"The outside is big," rumbled the reply. "You think this place where we live is

66

big but it's not. Outside there are more buildings just like it. More than you can count, and they go on forever."

"With lots of corridors in between!" added the squeaky voice.

"Roads," corrected the big one. "They're called roads. And that's where the danger is. Humans go on the roads in their cars, very fast. We were nearly spotted a few times."

"And we nearly got lost. We had to run," added the squeaky one. "But nobody saw us!"

"Very good, you did well," said the sharp voice, coming closer to Marlin. "But now — the main thing is we've caught him."

Something prodded Marlin's leg. He scrambled to his feet. He felt bruised but he had no broken bones.

"Well? What have you done with it?"

A light came on and Marlin squinted in the sudden brightness, trying to see.

A giant shadow leaned over him, armour plates towering up like jagged rocks. It was the creature with the sharp voice — it was the Stegosaurus. The T-Rex stood behind

him, leaning in close.

"I don't know what you mean…" protested Marlin.

"Don't you? Really?" snapped the Stegosaurus. "Follow me!"

He turned and flicked his spiked-tail. Then he marched across the room. The others crowded after him, herding Marlin between them.

There, standing in the shadows, was Protos.

Marlin ran over to him. But the old Centrosaurus was frozen still, his head bowed and his eyes closed.

"We want to know where Protos's battery is – where is the battery that *you* stole?"

Chapter Ten

·················

The Thief!

Marlin stood there and the dinosaurs crowded around, their metal plates rattling as they jostled to see him.

"Well?" demanded the Stegosaurus. "What have you got to say?"

Marlin looked up at them all – and he felt very small standing there. He felt himself trembling. But suddenly he realised that he wasn't frightened. No, he wasn't afraid – he was actually feeling angry. After all his hard work, this just wasn't fair!

"Now listen to me and stop talking!" he exclaimed. "I'm not a thief. I'm here to help you!"

The Stegosaurus took a step back,

frowning.

The other Dinoteks backed away too, all except the T-Rex. He squinted suspiciously at Marlin.

"Now then! Don't try any tricks," he growled. "Just answer the question."

"I'm not tricking you," said Marlin. "It is true I took all your batteries, but only to power them up. Then I brought them all back. They were in that bag."

He pointed across the room. The cloth bag was still on the floor exactly where he'd left it.

"Hmm... I did find all your batteries in that bag," growled the T-Rex.

"He could be telling the truth I suppose..."

"So if he's telling the truth, where is Protos's battery now?" demanded the Steg.

"Where I left it, of course," answered Marlin.

He went over to the bag and snatched it up. But it was empty.

"I don't understand..."

He looked at the metal creatures.

70

"Somebody else must have taken it!"

The Stegosaurus snorted. But the T-Rex stepped forward. He pushed his great nose down and sniffed at the bag.

"Maybe you're right," he said. "I *can* smell something else. Another human…"

Marlin suddenly had an idea. And it seemed such a definite idea that he was sure he was right about it.

There was only one person who could have come in here: Oliver Grubbler!

The T-Rex was sniffing, trying to catch the scent, to follow it.

"The trail leads this way…"

He paced across the room to stand by the window.

"Somewhere over there," he said grimly. "It's a long way off…"

They crowded round him and looked out into the dark. Far away, over the rooftops of the city, was a single building standing higher than all the others.

It was a great glass tower.

******

"**I** can see the battery!" exclaimed Dacky suddenly, making everyone jump.

"What?!" snapped Steg.

"At the top of that tower! There's a room. I can see humans, lots of them, all sitting around a table – and they have the battery, right there!"

"Nobody can see that far," snorted Steg.

"I can," cawed Dacky. "Superior vision is a well-known power of the Pterosaurs."

He unfurled his wings, and shook them. They stretched wide, filling half the room, like the sails of a great ship.

"I also have speed," he said. "So watch! Now I will fly to the glass tower and get the battery!"

He strode forwards, beat his wings – once, twice – and tripped over. His silver body sprawled awkwardly on the floor.

******

The T-Rex leaned down to help him. "You can't really fly, Dacky, remember?" he said gently. "Don't worry,

I'll go outside again."

"I...I wanted to help..." cawed the winged reptile, struggling to his feet

"You did help," said Flame. "Thanks to your eyes I now know exactly where to go. Comp and Siggy will help me." The two Troodons gave an excited squeak. The T-Rex strode over to the door and they scampered close behind him.

"But be careful," Steg snapped after them. "This could be very dangerous. Remember you're not going out into quiet roads. This time you're going right into the middle of the city and if the humans see you, they'll try to hunt you."

"We'll be careful," said Flame, grimly.

One of little Troodons nodded – was that one Siggy? – but the other looked nervous.

All of Dinoteks had forgotten about Marlin, who was still standing holding the empty bag.

He stepped forward.

"Wait!" he called. "I can help!"

******

Flame, the golden-headed T-Rex, looked down at Marlin.

"You want to help us? But you're so small," he growled. "And you're not even dressed properly."

It was true. Marlin was beginning to feel quite cold.

"Hah!" cawed Dacky. "I can fix that."

He flapped across the room and a moment later came back with a big bundle clutched in his beak. He dropped it at Marlin's feet.

"There! It's from my favourite part of the museum, the Flight Gallery."

Marlin unwrapped the bundle. It was a leather pilot's jacket. It was certainly large, made for an adult, but it might just fit. He tried it, and it did, hanging almost to his knees. It was lined with wool and it felt snug and warm. And there was a pair of goggles to pull over his eyes.

"I'll look like an old-fashioned racing driver," he laughed putting them on.

"Good. Because you'll be going fast," answered Flame.

And before   Marlin could argue, the   T-Rex bent down, picked him up, and threw him into the air.

It must have been a very skilful throw because Marlin somersaulted and landed perfectly on the great creature's back. He gasped and held out his arms to keep his balance.

"Look in front of you," Steg called up to him.

Marlin looked down at the T-Rex's back and at first saw nothing. Then he spotted it: a leather strap with a buckle.

"Undo the buckle and lift up the flap," ordered Steg.

Marlin did it. Underneath the flap there was a small space in the T-Rex's back, like

the cockpit of an aeroplane. And there, inside it, was a seat!

"In you pop," chuckled Flame. "It'll be much better than carrying you in my mouth. And this time we'll be able to talk to each other!"

Marlin grinned and slipped down into the seat. He did feel like a racing driver now, but this was going to be much better than riding in a car.

He was about to go racing on a T-Rex.

Chapter Eleven

· · · · · · · · · · · · · · · ·

Faster, Faster, FASTER!

The wind rushed past with a roar, catching Marlin's breath.

He pulled the racing goggles on so he could face straight into it without blinking.

"WOAH!"

This was the most thrilling thing he'd ever done!

"Hold on tight!" called Flame.

He began the journey with two great strides – THUD! THUD! – then they left the museum behind and he picked up speed.

He leaned forwards, his head dropped low and he began to accelerate. Then his legs became a blur.

Behind them, the two little Troodons skittered along, racing to keep up but not quite managing it. And every few seconds Flame looked back. Each time he did, Marlin could feel him slow down for them.

Wow! How fast would this T-Rex go if he *wasn't* waiting for anyone?

They crossed the city in no time, keeping to quiet roads and ducking into the shadows whenever a car appeared.

They jumped over a fence and then ran across a park, between trees. Now they were running on open grass, across a hillside, with sky all around them.

Suddenly Marlin knew what it must have been like for the prehistoric Tyrannosaurs sprinting across the wide, endless plains of the Jurassic. He closed his eyes and it was as if he really was back in that other time. It was a feeling of such freedom and excitement that he wanted it to go on forever.

But already Flame was slowing down.

"There it is," the T-Rex nodded.

The glass tower was there, right in front

of them. Marlin stared up at it, glittering against the sky. Now it looked huge.

It was brightly lit, and all the area around it was lit-up too – there was a car park in front, but it was empty of cars.

"Hmmm…there's nowhere here to hide here," muttered Flame.

"Yes there is, look!" replied Marlin.

On the far side, half in shadow, was a grassy bank. Flame nodded.

"Good, let's get over there and out of sight."

The Troodons followed and they all huddled together and looked up at the tower.

"What now?" squeaked Comp.

Marlin suddenly felt nervous. Now they'd arrived he didn't know what to do – only that this was the most important part of the mission.

"I'll go," he said.

Flame nodded.

"Good. I think it's a job for a human. But be careful. Get in and out as fast as you can."

Marlin climbed out of the seat and slid down the T-Rex's tail. He turned towards the tower. This was it.

******

The way in was through a glass door. On the other side of the glass Marlin could see there was a desk…and a chair…and sitting there, a man in a uniform. It was the building's security guard – and he looked big.

What now? He'll never let me inside…

But suddenly he had an idea! He called over his shoulder.

"Siggy? Can you do that trick again, like you did on me? Can you get the guard to come out?"

The Troodon blinked and nodded. And his tail wagged happily.

******

The security guard's name was Buster Crank. His two favourite treats in life were breaking things and eating sausages.

He only broke things if he was allowed
to break them (which didn't happen very
often) but at least he had sausages every day.
He liked all sorts, even vegetarian ones.

He was thinking about sausages when
something silver flashed past outside. He
saw it, just for a second, then it was gone.

He frowned and tried to get back to
thinking about sausages. He thought about
how nice they
smelled when they
were sizzling in his
pan...how cosy they
sounded as they
crackled...how good
they tasted when he
took the first bite...

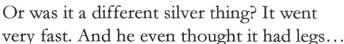

But then the
silver thing went past
again.

Or was it a different silver thing? It went
very fast. And he even thought it had legs...

"Right! I'd better go and look."

He got up and opened the glass door.

He stepped outside and peered around. He pointed with his torch. But he couldn't see the silver thing at all now.

"Very strange that is…"

He didn't notice the young boy slipping through the door behind him.

******

Marlin got into the lift. It was new and shiny and the doors closed with a gentle swish. He looked at all the buttons, then pressed the highest number, hoping that would take him to the top floor.

Up he went.

The doors hissed open again and he stepped out into an empty corridor. There were doors on both sides, all closed. But right ahead he could hear voices talking. And there was one door, just open a crack.

He crept closer and suddenly he saw it. The battery was inside that room – Protos's battery!

It was so close he could almost reach it.

But the room was full of people. They were having a big meeting. And it was going to be a long meeting because there was a tea trolley next to the door, loaded with nice things to eat and drink.

He thought about what to do.

He could just rush in and grab the battery.

Or he could creep in quietly, keeping low and hope nobody noticed. They were all so busy talking that he might just get away with it.

Or he might not.

His heart was beating fast and his mouth had gone dry. He really didn't want to go into that room with all those people but he knew he must.

He remembered Protos's words – "I'm glad it was *you* Marlin…"

Thinking of the Centrosaurus made him more determined. And suddenly he had an idea.

******

The tea trolley was next to the door, piled up with cups, saucers, pots of tea and a big plate of chocolate biscuits. Before he could change his mind Marlin grabbed the trolley and wheeled it straight into the room.

"Tea anyone?" he announced cheerfully.

Everyone stopped talking and looked at him, puzzled. For a horrible moment Marlin thought somebody would demand to know who he was. But he carried on with his act and began putting cups and saucers on the table.

It worked.

One by one the eyes turned away from him. The talking began again.

"Yes, yes" sniffed a man at one end of the table. "I agree with Mr Grubbler. Let's sell them…"

Marlin worked his way around the table – cup, saucer, cup, saucer – and was careful not to look at anyone.

"…do you know how much money we'd get for them?"

Cup, saucer, cup, saucer…

"A very good question," agreed a grey-haired man (*the Mayor?*). "We should certainly try for the best price…"

Marlin had gone right round the table and so far his plan was working well. But the next part would be the hardest. He wheeled the trolley towards Grubbler and the battery.

"I've made a few phone calls," Grubbler was saying. "And nobody wants them as they are. It's not surprising, they don't look very good. I almost gave up. But then I called Mr Snickenbacker…"

"The scrap metal millionaire?"

"Yes, that's right…"

Marlin put a cup in front of Grubbler

and felt the cold battery brush the back of his hand…

"Snickenbacker's offering a very good price…"

This was it. Time for Marlin to try his plan. He picked up the plate of biscuits and slid it into the middle of the table.

Immediately, all eyes were on it, and people began leaning forward greedily, reaching out for a biscuit. In that same moment Marlin scooped up the battery and turned for the door.

"Yes," continued Grubbler, now chomping noisily. "He said he'll buy them and break them up for scrap. That's the only thing those old dinosaurs are good for."

Marlin froze. *Dinosaurs? — the Dinoteks! —* that's what these people were talking about and he hadn't realised it!

"No! You can't!" he gasped. "You can't sell them for scrap!"

And then everyone looked at him.

"You!" roared Grubbler, jumping to his feet.

Marlin shoved the tea trolley at him and ran.

Chapter Twelve

················

The Wrong Way Stairs

"What's happening now? What can you see?" demanded Steg.

Dacky was peering at the tower,

telling them what Marlin was doing.
Suddenly he gasped, flapping his wings wide
with alarm.

"What's wrong? What is it?!"

"It's the boy!" the Pterosaur cawed.
"They're chasing him!"

******

Marlin sprinted down the corridor and
Grubbler's heavy footsteps thundered
behind him. He was getting closer.

"Stop you little thief! Give that back!"

But Marlin held tightly on to the battery.

He threw himself to one side just as
Grubbler was about to grab him.

Marlin stopped sharply but Grubbler
couldn't! He was bigger
and heavier and went
crashing on down the
corridor.

Marlin doubled
back and pushed open a door.
Stairs – but they were leading
the wrong way, upwards,

not down!
He had no
choice but
to go up.
Grubbler
was coming
again and
now Marlin
could hear
more shouts
too as others
joined the
chase. He

dashed up the stairs two at a time and threw
himself through another door at the top.

Cold night air hit him. He looked about,
confused. Then he realised where he was:
on the roof! The lights of the city were
shining all around him and below him. Up
here on top of the
tower he was above
everything.

*Quick! Find
another way out...*

He sprinted

across the flat open roof, looking around, but there were no other doors.

He reached the edge.

Far below in the car park he could see the golden-headed T-Rex pacing up and down and the Troodons beside him. They were tiny but even from this far away Flame still looked big.

Marlin thought about calling out to him. But, for all the T-Rex's size and speed, what would he be able to do from down there?

He looked at the battery and looked down to the ground. Maybe he could throw it down? Maybe Flame could catch it?

But what if it breaks?!

"Hah! Got you!"

Grubbler came crashing through the door onto the roof. He stood there for a moment just grinning, then he rushed forwards.

******

"He's trapped! Caught!"

Dacky had been watching Marlin on the roof and he saw Grubbler attack. Now he lifted his head and cawed at the sky in despair.

He shook his useless wings – and at that very moment the wind blew.

The wind blew and it lifted him.

Suddenly he was being carried upwards on a cushion of air and he felt like he was a tiny leaf being blown away into a huge sky.

He felt lost.

But a moment later Steg's voice reached him, calling up from far below, encouraging him.

"You're doing great Dacky! Keep flying! Use your wings!"

Dacky did. He beat downwards. He felt himself lift. He tilted his wings and felt himself turn. He swooped down then looped up again.

Now he wasn't a leaf being blown away, now he was flying – he was a Pterosaur, he was a master of the air!

"Aaaak! Aaaak!"

Dacky knew what he had to do.

He flew straight across the city.

He soared above the streets, sailed across the green hill and swooped down between the tall buildings.

The tall glass tower came into sight. He could see Marlin on the roof. The big man had hold of him and was dragging him in through a doorway. There was no time to think.

Dacky swooped.

******

"That's an end to your little game!" snarled Grubbler giving Marlin's

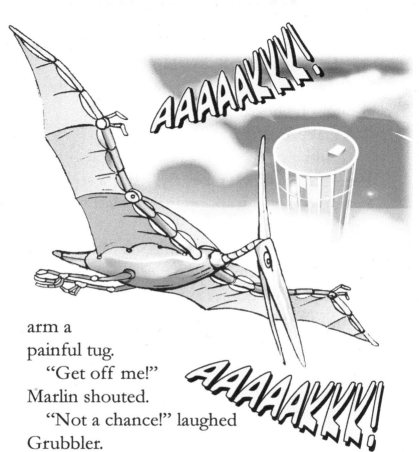

AAAAAKKK!

arm a
painful tug.

"Get off me!"
Marlin shouted.

"Not a chance!" laughed
Grubbler.

AAAAAAKKK!

He had the door open now. He was
holding it with his foot and pulling Marlin
inside.

BANG!

The door slammed shut behind them and
Marlin felt himself trapped.

"Got you now!" gloated Grubbler.

But in that very last moment, before

the door had closed, Marlin thought he
saw something swooping overhead and he
thought he heard a cry.

"Aaak! Aaaak!"

Could it be?! No, it was impossible – the
Pterosaur couldn't really fly...But a strange
feeling of hope leapt up inside Marlin and
that gave him strength.

He kicked Grubbler's shin very hard and
pulled his arm free.

"Aargh!" Grubbler roared in fury and
Marlin dived backwards through the door.

He fell onto the roof and tried to
scramble away but Grubbler was straight
onto him, grabbing with his powerful arms.

Marlin was lifted – but now it was Dacky
who had hold of him, not Grubbler!

"Hold on boy!" the creature shouted.

His great wings beat down – once, twice
three times – and the force of the wind
knocked Grubbler off his feet.

Marlin and Dacky soared away and
the furious man stared after them, too
astonished even to speak.

Chapter Thirteen

·······················

A Bad Man Makes his Plans

Grubbler didn't stay lying down for long.

He sprinted down the stairs and bumped into the Mayor and the city councillors coming up.

"Did you catch him?" panted the Mayor. "What happened?"

But Grubbler shoved past him.

"Back down!" he snapped. "And somebody call the police! One of those things has come to life and it's flying around."

The Mayor ran after him.

"Come to life? What do you mean?"

"I mean one of the machines. It's got out of the museum and it attacked me. You know what that means?"

The Mayor looked at him, confused.

"Well, I er…"

"It means that if one of the machines can escape, they all can!" snapped Grubbler.

He dived into the lift and pulled the Mayor in after him.

"We've got to bring the plan forward."

"Well yes, I suppose…do you think we should have another meeting?…"

But Grubbler ignored him. He was thinking hard.

"Listen," he snapped as the lift raced downwards towards the ground floor. "Here's what we'll do. I'll call Snickenbacker at once. He's got lots of people and lots of trucks. They can go straight to the museum and start pulling the monsters apart before it's too late."

"Oh yes, pull the monsters apart," agreed the Mayor. "We don't like monsters…"

PING!

The lift arrived and Grubbler stormed out.

Dacky landed on the grass close to where Flame was waiting with the Troodons. It wasn't the smoothest landing. Marlin went rolling over, clutching the precious battery to his chest.

Dacky sprawled on his front and his wings scraped along in the mud. But the crash landing didn't bother the Troodons.

"You can fly! You can fly!" they squeaked, running over to help him up.

"It's quite easy," shrugged Dacky. "Nothing to get excited about..."

But really he was very pleased with himself.

Flame looked down at Marlin.

"What happened?"

"I got it," nodded Marlin, holding up the battery. "But they nearly caught me. Dacky arrived just in time."

Flame turned to the others.

"Well done everyone!" he called. "But I don't think we should stay here too long..."

Even as he spoke, they heard voices shouting in the distance and the sound of a police siren came wailing across the city, getting louder.

"Dacky – can you fly again?"

"Of course," sniffed the Pterosaur.

"Then go! Fly straight back to the museum and take the battery."

"Certainly."

Dacky hopped over and took the cylinder from Marlin. As he did so he lowered his great beak.

"Well done boy," he said. "You were very brave."

Marlin grinned up at him.

"Goodbye!" called Dacky. Then he turned into the wind, stretched his wings and was gone.

"You too, little ones!" called Flame. "Run as fast as you can, straight back the way we came!"

The Troodons hopped over to Marlin.

"Well done boy," they both said. "You were very brave."

"Thank you," said Marlin.

Then they turned and darted away into the shadows with a laugh.

"Now us," smiled Flame.

And he picked Marlin
up – gently this time –
and lowered him onto his
back. Marlin slipped down
into the seat.

"Ready Marlin?"
"Ready Flame!"
And they were off.

Marlin leaned back and
tried to catch sight of
Dacky in the sky, but he
was already gone. Now
there were only stars,

passing steadily by as they raced along.

"You did well," said Flame. "Tell me what happened up in the tower."

"They were having a meeting," began Marlin – and he told the T-Rex what he had discovered.

Flame grunted.

"Scrap metal, eh?"

"Yes! We've got to do something," Marlin replied. "Or they'll try to take you away."

"Don't worry," replied Flame. "I'm sure we'll be fine. Protos will be back with us soon and he'll know what to do."

And he sounded so certain that Marlin believed what he said and settled back in his seat. He yawned, suddenly exhausted from his adventure.

Yes, Protos was very wise. He would know what to do...

And then Marlin discovered that riding in a safe seat, high up on the back of a friendly T-Rex, is the perfect way to fall asleep.

******

Far away, in a very big house on the other side of the city, Howard H. Snickenbacker was also asleep – but at that moment he was woken by an urgent buzzing sound.

BUZZZ...BUZZZ...BUZZZ...

He sat up, grumbling, and fumbled for his phone.

"Yes? Who?!" he snapped. "Grubbler? This had better be important!"

It was pitch black in Snickenbacker's bedroom, far too dark to see – but if it had been a bit lighter, and if you had been able to see his face, you would certainly not have liked the greedy smile that was now slowly spreading across it.

It was the smile of a predator that had not had a good meal for a long time and had just smelled something interesting.

"I see...yes I understand...well that shouldn't be a problem."

Snickenbacker snapped the phone off and slipped smoothly out of his bed, his expensive silk pyjamas hissing, snake-like, over the sheets.

He walked across the bedroom – it was very large, because he was very rich – to the window. And he reached out a hand to the curtains.

Below him, in the yard, his army was waiting.

It was an army of diggers and bulldozers and giant trucks covered with claws and hooks. They were all painted black, and looked like a colony of gigantic insects. Sleeping insects. But soon to be woken.

Snickenbacker picked up his phone again.

"Smith? It's me. Wake up the men – we're going hunting."

The end of Book One
(Book Two begins on page 113)

Marlin's Dinotek notebook

Some of the Dinoteks...

Comp and Siggy

Whip-tail essential for balance

At first it can be hard to tell the two Troodons apart - but their faces are slightly different. They are both very sweet (also a bit naughty).

Their claws are good at gripping

Comp is a bit more sensible (but only sometimes).

Main skills
- dodging
- hiding
- escaping
- playing tricks
- night-vision

Top running speed? Not sure - but they're second fastest after Flame.

The first of his kind...

Protos

Protos is the OLDEST of the Dinoteks - and he seems to be very clever.
He stayed awake the longest after the Professor vanished. When I woke Protos it was quite sad because he didn't realise how many years he had slept.

I found his worn out battery hidden here.

A real Centrosaurus in the Late Cretaceous Period.

These herbivores roamed the Earth 75 million years ago.

CHARGE!

Protos has one horn (not three like a Triceratops).
One of his legs doesn't work well - but he has tough armour.
I think he would be able to DEFEND himself!

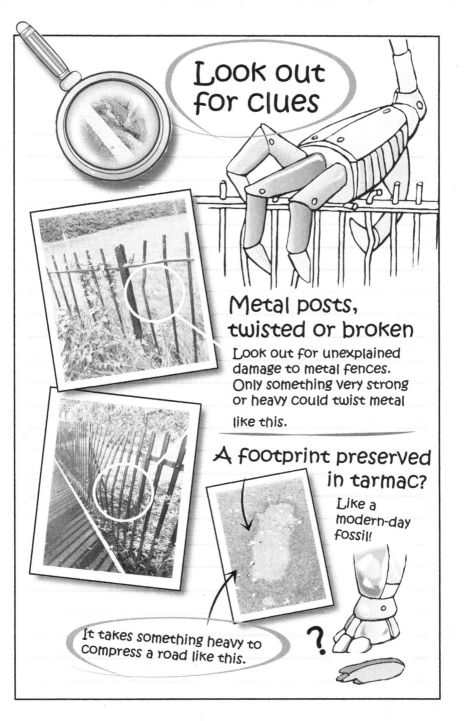

Signs of dino-damage

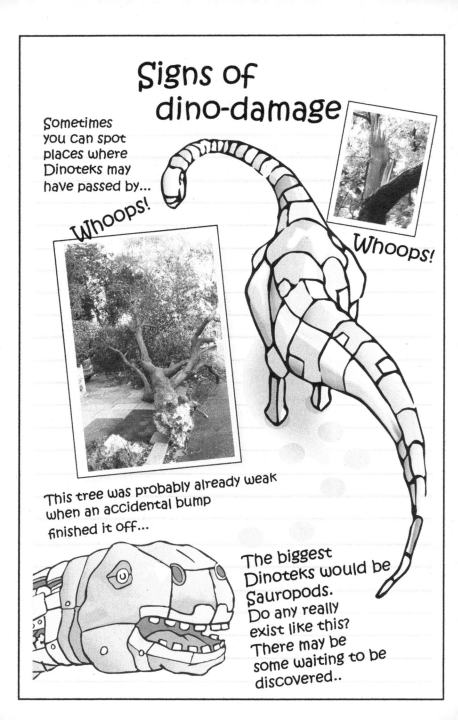

Sometimes you can spot places where Dinoteks may have passed by...

Whoops!

Whoops!

This tree was probably already weak when an accidental bump finished it off...

The biggest Dinoteks would be Sauropods. Do any really exist like this? There may be some waiting to be discovered..

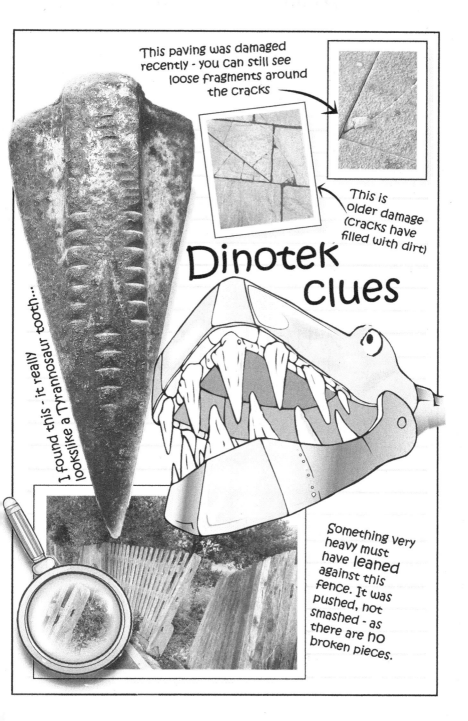

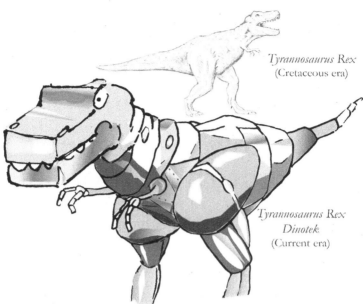

Tyrannosaurus Rex
(Cretaceous era)

Tyrannosaurus Rex Dinotek
(Current era)

The Secret Dinosaur Hunters Attack

Centrosaurus
(Cretaceous era)

Centrosaurus Dinotek
(Current era)

A mystery

· · · · · · · · · · · · · ·

How everyone forgot the Dinoteks

It was supposed to happen like this: the mechanical dinosaur was supposed to wait for visitors at the museum entrance.

"Welcome," he would say. "My name is Protos. Come with me and let's imagine that we are travelling back through time, back to the world of the dinosaurs…"

And then Protos was supposed to take the visitors into a room full of living machine dinosaurs – Dinoteks, every bit as fantastic as he was.

But it didn't happen.

Something went wrong.

The Professor who had created

the Dinoteks disappeared and in their room at the museum, one by one, the creatures fell asleep. Their batteries failed and they froze where they were, becoming just metal statues.

Protos was the last one left awake.

He looked out of the museum window expecting any moment to see the Professor hurrying up the steps clutching his bag full of papers and gadgets and special tools.

Protos watched and waited. And after a whole day he went to stand in his little room next to the Dinosaur Gallery.

"I'll just practise my speech," he said to himself. "Ahem! Ladies and gentlemen, girls and boys, imagine travelling back in time to the Jurassic era. Close your eyes and picture it. A hundred million years seems like a long time but really it's just the blink of an eye… really, just the blink of an…"

And with one last yawn his head nodded and Protos slept too.

****

Many years passed and gradually everybody forgot about the Dinoteks. Dust settled on them, burying them like fossils.

The door to their room was no longer opened and its hinges became stiff with rust.

New models arrived at the museum, made of plastic not metal. They weren't alive, but they looked much more realistic.

People stopped coming into the little room to look at Protos.

They thought he was rather funny – just an odd looking statue made out of scraps of metal.

Until one day Marlin Maxton arrived...

Clunk!

Chapter One

....

The Silent
Visitor

The creature was so big that its head easily reached up to the top floor of the house.

It arrived in the middle of the

night, stepping over the garden fence, and nobody saw it.

The house had three windows upstairs and the creature seemed to know exactly which one it was looking for.

It leaned down and nudged the edge of the wooden frame. The window opened and the creature lifted something from its back and lowered it into the house.

A moment later it was gone, slipping into the mist like a ghost, as silently and quickly as it had arrived.

There was no sign that it had ever been there, except in the grass underneath the window.

Pressed down very deep in the lawn was a massive, three-toed footprint.

****

Marlin Maxton woke up to find himself in bed the wrong way round.

His trainers were still on his feet and the window was wide open.

The coat he was wearing wasn't his. It

was three sizes too big and it had been given to him by a dinosaur. Well not a dinosaur exactly, a Dinotek…

Marlin rolled over and rubbed his head.

However could he explain all this to anyone?

It was all so amazing, so incredible, they'd think he was making it up.

They would laugh!

Or worse, they might scream. Because they might think the Dinoteks were dangerous…

Marlin sat up.

Dangerous…

He had suddenly remembered something very important from last night.

He jumped out of bed.

He had to get help – and there was only one person in the world who would listen.

****

Marlin sprinted down the back garden and along the alleyway between the houses.

There, tucked away among a tangle of

bushes was a little brick building with a patched-up metal roof. It was Uncle Gus' workshop.

It was built against the side of an oak tree and a tyre hung from a rope that was looped over one of the tree's branches. Marlin and Uncle Gus had tied it up there last summer and he had spent lazy afternoons swinging from it, reading.

No time for reading now though...

As he sprinted along the alley Marlin was glad to hear hammering sounds from inside the little building. Uncle Gus was in.

****

The old man sat quietly as Marlin told his whole story. He nodded from time to time but didn't speak.

They were perched together on the sofa and Uncle Gus was sipping from a big mug of tea. Steam curled up through his bushy eyebrows and made him look like a wizard.

Marlin was holding a mug of tea as well but he was too busy talking to drink anything.

He told
Uncle Gus
how the
Dinoteks had
finally come
back to life.

He grabbed
a sheet of
paper and drew
a sketch to
show just how
impressive the T-Rex was.

Uncle Gus leaned forwards and added
some notes of his own to the picture as
Marlin talked.

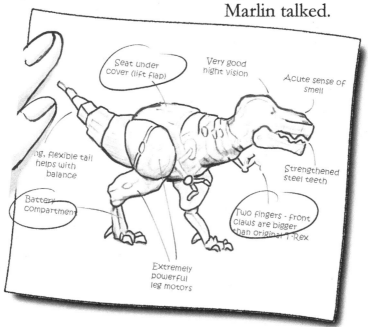

He was very interested in machines.

"Yes, yes, I can see he'd be fast this one... it's a nice design, lad, very nice... and what's this?"

He pointed to the creature's back. Marlin nodded. That was the best thing of all!

The T-Rex had a special, hidden seat on his back. And last night the creature had picked him up in its teeth, flipped him through the air, and caught him very carefully so he'd landed right next to the seat.

"It's very safe and you can ride on him. It's like... like the world's best roller coaster!"

"Ah! That sounds fabulous lad, I do love a good roller coaster. I remember there used to be one down at the sea front. Lovely mechanism it had..."

Marlin's face changed.

"But Uncle, there's trouble too. The museum manager hates the Dinoteks – he wants to destroy them and turn them into scrap metal. I've done my best to help but Protos is still asleep and I don't know what to do next..."

Marlin waited to see what his uncle would say.

Uncle Gus had put down his mug and was pacing up and down, frowning.

Marlin looked up at him.

"What do you think, Uncle?"

Uncle Gus stopped pacing – and suddenly headed for the back of his workshop.

"Two things lad," he called. "Two things…"

His voice was muffled because now he was rummaging inside a cupboard.

He emerged, holding a rucksack.

"First, I think you are about to have a very important adventure."

He passed Marlin the rucksack.

"I had this packed for you, just in case. I've put in some tools, some food and – Ah!"

Suddenly he clapped his hand to his head.

"I nearly forgot!"

He dashed over to his workbench and grabbed a golden box to give Marlin.

"The battery charger!" said Marlin.

"Exactly, lad! Just in case the Dinoteks run low. About twenty minutes for each battery should be enough."

Marlin stuffed the golden box into the rucksack.

"What's the second thing?" he asked.

"Eh?"

"You said there were two things Uncle!"

"Did I? Ah yes! The second thing is this lad – you need a *plan*."

****

Five minutes later Marlin saw something that he'd never seen before, and never really thought that he ever would.

Uncle Gus pushed his old car out of the workshop and started up the engine.

It had been in there for so long, in pieces, that Marlin didn't think it would ever actually work.

But it did.

The engine chugged a bit at first, but then it settled into a steady, rumbling purr.

Marlin grinned. It was a great sound!

They jumped into the car and headed for the museum.

Chapter Two

· · · · · · · · · · · · · · · ·

The Creature on
the Lawn

A crow was hopping across the lawn in front of the museum, looking for something to eat. This was a good place to hunt because people often dropped scraps of food here – but suddenly the crow stopped and raised its head. It listened for a moment then it spread its black wings and flew off.

It had a bad feeling.

Something was coming.

****

A minute later another creature arrived. It looked around warily, checking for danger, then it hurried across the grass to stand under a tree.

This was a good place to hide.

From here you could look across the open square to the museum and see everything that was going on.

And today, a lot would be happening here.

The creature was fully grown and quite large.

Its name was Oliver Grubbler.

Grubbler was the museum manager.

He lifted a pair of binoculars to his eyes and scanned the building.

Nothing. No sign of life.

But Grubbler wasn't fooled. He knew they were in there somewhere.

He thought about moving closer but decided not to. The Dinoteks must not see him. When the attack on the museum began – very soon now – it had to be a total surprise.

"Mr Grubbler!" called a voice.

He looked up to see a man in a grey suit hurrying across the lawn towards him. It was the Mayor.

"Have you seen them again? Have you seen the monsters?"

"Not yet," whispered Grubbler.

The Mayor glanced at the museum. He was sweating nervously. He pulled out a tissue and wiped his brow.

"And you're sure? The monsters are definitely in there?"

"I'm certain," Grubbler replied. "They're hiding inside. But they won't be able to hide for long. Not once my friends get

here…"

And at exactly that moment, as the museum clock struck ten, Howard H. Snickenbacker and his Demolition Army arrived.

****

S nickenbacker's Demolition Army appeared like this: the first thing to arrive was a truck.

Just a truck. There was nothing unusual about it, except for its colour. It was completely black, from the top of its cabin to the bottom of its chunky wheels.

Next came a jeep and there was nothing very odd about that either except that it was bigger than usual and also totally black.

But the things that came after, well they were *very* strange.

Some of the vehicles looked like diggers, and others like bulldozers, but most were strange mix-up machines with lots of odd pieces joined together. They had hooks and chains and gigantic snapping claws.

All of them were painted the same shiny black and, as they came into the square one after another, they looked like a colony of gigantic, lumbering beetles.

Grubbler watched them roll forwards and he smiled as he felt the air rumbling and roaring. It was a good sound. A powerful sound.

They crunched their way across the road, then

trundled up onto the lawn in front of the museum and began to line up in rows.

The Mayor looked anxiously at the neat grass and the beautiful flower beds as the wheels rolled over them.

"Oh dear...I hope they don't make too much mess Mr Grubbler..."

But Grubbler wasn't listening. He was staring through his binoculars again waiting for the attack on the museum to begin.

Neither Grubbler nor the Mayor noticed when one small vehicle arrived late.

****

Uncle Gus parked by the edge of the grass.

"It looks like we're just in time lad…"

In front of them the black trucks and diggers were still lining up. Uncle Gus tutted and shook his head.

"Just look at them all…"

"Don't worry, I'll get past them Uncle!"

Marlin heaved the rucksack from the back seat and slipped it onto his back.

"You know what to do lad?"

"Yes," said Marlin.

"Ready?"

"Ready!" – and he gave his uncle a hug before opening the door and jumping out.

A moment later Uncle Gus revved up the little car's engine. He drove up onto the grass and began chugging around in circles, weaving in and out among the neat rows of diggers. The drivers in their black uniforms looked at him, puzzled. Some of them began to shout at him but Uncle Gus just honked his horn and waved cheerfully.

Round and round he went.

Marlin took his chance.

While everyone was looking the other way he set off across the grass towards the museum.

He walked very calmly – *just look as if you belong here* – and nobody noticed him. He got right across the lawn and ducked into the side road next to the museum.

Easy, he grinned.

Now he just had to work out how to get inside.

Chapter Three

· · · · · · · · · · · · · · ·

The Only Way In

Marlin sneaked into the road beside the museum and looked up at the impressive stone building. One of the windows was open.

He was certain that he could squeeze through it. But first he had to reach it. It was on the first floor.

The front of the museum was very beautiful. It was covered with carvings of plants and animals. But on this side of the building there were no ornaments, nothing to hang on to.

Except for one thing – a crooked cast-iron drainpipe was fixed to the wall. As it snaked upwards, it went close to the window. It looked sturdy enough to climb.

Marlin looked at it.

High up, there were connections running out from the sides of the pipe like branches from a tree. And climbing trees was easy.

Marlin smiled.

But at that moment a large man in a uniform came lumbering towards him.

****

It was Buster Crank the security guard. Buster was a big man and he swayed from side to side as he walked. But he hadn't noticed Marlin. No, he was thinking about the mysterious events of last night.

Last night.

Hmmm...

He scratched his head and tried to work it out.

Something very odd had happened to Buster while he was guarding the Glass Tower. First there had been the strange silver thing – he had seen it, he had definitely seen it. And then there was the clever thief.

Yes. Buster had got into big trouble over that. Mr Grubbler had shouted at him.

Somehow a thief had got past him and into the building.

But how had that happened?

Buster pondered.

And then he looked up and noticed Marlin walking towards him. The boy had a heavy bag on his back and his hands were stuffed into his pockets.

He didn't *look* like a criminal – but today Buster had to be especially careful.

"What are you up to?" he demanded.

"I was just wondering," replied the boy.

"Wondering what?"

And the boy pointed upwards, above Buster's head.

"Should that window be open? I mean, couldn't someone get in?"

Buster looked up.

"You're right!"

He stretched up, but couldn't reach the window. He jumped, but didn't get very far.

Too many sausages this morning Buster, he thought.

"That's no use," said the boy, shaking his head. "Would you like me to help?"

Buster looked at him.

"Would you?"

The boy nodded.

"See that drainpipe? Give me a hand up. I'm sure I could climb it."

"A good plan," nodded Buster.

He knelt on one knee and helped the boy to clamber up.

The boy was quick. He shimmied up the drainpipe to reach the window.

"Careful!" called Buster.

"OK," said the boy as he pulled himself onto the ledge. "Nearly there…"

Then he disappeared through the window and – BANG – he shut it from

inside.

Buster nodded, satisfied. Now the building was totally secure.

He carried on his patrol, along the road, and as he went he smiled.

Nobody would get past him today.

Chapter Four

· · · · · · · · · · · · · · ·

Friends
Meet Again

Marlin sprinted through the empty corridors and his footsteps echoed in the silence. The museum was deserted now but he knew that it would soon be full of people. In his mind he pictured the Dinoteks being surrounded and dragged outside in chains. Even Flame, with his legs tangled, would be pulled down and taken.

No! That must not happen!

He sprang down a staircase three steps at a time, ran into the museum entrance hall and crashed straight into the T-Rex.

"Woah!"

Flame looked down amazed.

"Marlin! What are you doing here? You're supposed to be at home!"

"I came to find *you*," replied Marlin, picking himself up. "Why did you leave me behind? I told you, I'm going to help you!"

The T-Rex snorted and shook his head.

"It's kind of you to try but what I really need here is another T-Rex. Or a whole family of them…"

And he looked out through the glass doors. All morning he had been watching as the black vehicles got closer. Now a massive bulldozer had rumbled up with smoke billowing from its exhaust pipe.

"I'm sure it won't be long now," he muttered to himself. "They're moving in…"

"But where's Protos?" exclaimed Marlin. "And all the others?"

"Upstairs," answered Flame. "They're still trying to wake Protos but it's not working."

He sighed and shook his head.

"I think there must be something wrong with his battery. Marlin, do you think – Marlin?!"

But Marlin had already gone.

S teg couldn't think of what to do next.
He could see the others watching him
– Dacky and the little ones – and he knew
how much they wanted Protos to wake up.
He wanted it too.

"I'll just try it one more time the other
way," he said.

"But you've already tried that three
times!" squeaked Siggy.

"I know!" snapped Steg. "But what else
can I do? It doesn't help with everyone
staring at me!"

Siggy hung his head and Steg immediately

felt bad.

"I'm sorry," he said. "I'm doing my best."

He reached into Protos' battery space — the compartment in his leg — and pulled the grey cylinder out again. He turned it over in his beak and pushed it back in, snapping the cover shut.

Nothing happened.

They all looked again at the old Centrosaurus. But there was no sign of life, none at all.

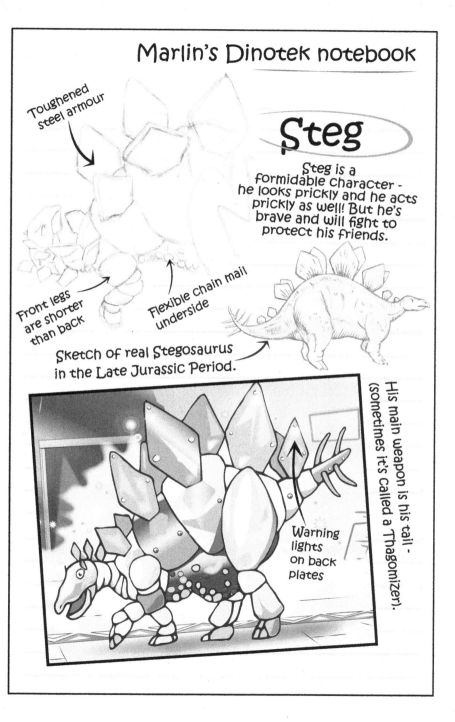

Marlin's Dinotek notebook

Toughened steel armour

Steg

Steg is a formidable character - he looks prickly and he acts prickly as well! But he's brave and will fight to protect his friends.

Front legs are shorter than back

Flexible chain mail underside

Sketch of real Stegosaurus in the Late Jurassic Period.

His main weapon is his tail - (sometimes it's called a Thagomizer).

Warning lights on back plates

Chapter Five

· · · · · · · · · · · · · · · ·

The Attack of the Demolition Army

"It's time," growled Grubbler.

Howard H. Snickenbacker was standing next to him on the museum steps, looking up at the glass doors.

Nothing moved. The air was still. Even the birds had stopped singing.

"Are you sure?" asked Snickenbacker.

"Yes," nodded Grubbler.

"Excellent. Then let's begin."

****

Marlin skidded into the secret room. "The battery," he shouted. "Put it in!"

Steg looked up.

"I did! It's not working!"

"It has to!"

Marlin dashed over and fell to his knees beside Protos' huge foot. His eyes scanned across the mechanical parts, desperately searching for the problem.

He remembered the very first day when he had accidentally brought the old creature back to life.

It was the first time he'd realised the Dinoteks were living machines. All he had done was fix a few loose parts – without even thinking. It had been so easy.

But now he felt panicked and he couldn't see at all what to do.

The battery was in its right place. There were no loose wires. There was one pin hanging out and he snapped it back, but that made no difference.

Then suddenly he heard the sound that he had been dreading. The sound of roaring engines from the front of the building.

"They're coming!" he exclaimed.

Steg snorted and his armour plates bristled angrily.

"We've got to help Flame. We must defend ourselves!"

And with a flick of his spear-covered tail he led the way to the door. Dacky and the Troodons went with him.

Marlin followed too.

He looked back one last time at Protos then he sprinted after the others towards the entrance hall where Flame was alone, facing the attack.

Chapter Six

·················

The Bulldozer

In a billow of smoke the massive bulldozer trundled up to the museum steps. It paused at the top.

Behind it, the others also came forwards, their engines revving. A digger lifted its black jaws – black, except for two rows of steel-grey teeth. They snapped hungrily in the air.

Oliver Grubbler lifted a megaphone to his mouth.

"Dinosaurs! Listen to me! You are ordered to leave the building immediately!"

His voice echoed harshly above the roar of the machines.

"You have one minute to surrender! Come out NOW or you will be destroyed!"

Then he began the countdown.

"Fifty nine...fifty eight...fifty seven..."

Inside the entrance hall Flame moved at last. He turned and stepped forwards.

Now he was standing directly in front of the doors and he could see that he was badly outnumbered. If he could just hold the first machine back – the bulldozer at the front – he might be able to block the way.

If...

The black machine looked strong. Flame was built for speed and he had powerful jaws but the bulldozer was made to push and to shove.

It would not stop.

Its caterpillar tracks would grip the ground firmly but Flame's clawed feet would scrape and slip on the polished tiles as he tried to hold his place.

He would be pushed backwards and then all the other machines would come in one after the other. They would surround him and attack together.

He knew this would happen unless he could think of something else to do.

Unless...

"We're here!" barked a voice behind him.

Steg powered into the hall.

****

The Stegosaurus' armour plates were shivering fiercely and his eyes flashed. Flame thought he looked suddenly bigger.

"Where do you want me?!" Steg snapped.

"Here," answered Flame, nodding to the empty space next to him.

The smaller Dinoteks crowded in now – Dacky, Comp, Siggy – and they made a second line behind the two giants.

And then Marlin skidded into the room. He looked around frantically.

What could he do to help?

Suddenly he saw what he needed!

There was a suit of armour next to the ticket desk and Marlin grabbed its shield. He took the sword too and lifted it above his head – it was long and heavy but felt good in his hand – then he went to stand in-between Flame and Steg.

Flame looked down at him, sternly.

"Marlin! You can't stand there, you might

get hurt!" he growled.

"Yes. That's a bad idea. Very bad indeed," said another voice.

It took all of them a moment to recognise who it was. Then they turned – Marlin, Flame and the others – to see Protos standing right behind them.

****

"Those bulldozers can be a bit rough," Protos said. "I wouldn't get in their way if I were you."

He turned and lumbered through a doorway at the back of the hall.

For a moment nobody moved – so amazed were they to see him that they even forgot about the people outside.

But then Grubbler's voice boomed louder.

"...twenty... nineteen... eighteen..."

Marlin shook himself.

"Come on everyone!"

He ran to catch up with Protos and the others all followed.

"You're back!" he exclaimed. "You're awake!"

"Yes and I'm so pleased to see you," the old creature chuckled.

Suddenly he stopped.

"Did you get into trouble with your teacher?"

Teacher? What was he talking about?!

Then Marlin remembered his school trip all those weeks ago. Protos had been asleep since then!

"No, I didn't get into trouble," he said.

"Oh that *is* a relief," nodded Protos.

And he set off again.

"I'm so glad everything's OK."

"But Protos you don't understand, they're going to…"

"You know I was quite worried about you. I thought you might get told off for being late. I remember once when – "

"Protos! Listen!"

The Centrosaurus stopped and turned to him.

"Wait a moment Marlin," he whispered. "First there's something important I need to tell you. Don't tell the others, I don't want to frighten them…"

"What is it?"

"All those bulldozers and diggers, did you notice them? I can't be totally sure but I think – I think they're planning something bad…"

"I know!" exclaimed Marlin. "That's what I've been trying to tell you! They're attacking us!"

"Really?"

"Yes!"

"Oh."

At that moment there was a loud crash behind them and the sound of glass shattering.

"Quick Protos, you've got to do something!"

Protos blinked and looked thoughtful for a moment. Then he nodded.

"You'd better follow me then…"

Chapter Seven

·················

A Room Full of Dinosaur Books

Now Protos moved surprisingly quickly.

He hurried through a series of long galleries, picking his way between display cabinets and exhibits.

They went through Dacky's favourite part of the museum, the Flight Gallery, and then headed down a long corridor.

Suddenly he stopped again.

"This is the best place to hide."

Marlin looked around. They were in a room full of books. On one wall there was a huge map of the world showing where different fossils had been found.

Steg pushed his way to the front.

"This isn't clever. We'll be trapped here!"
Flame nodded.

"He's right, it's not safe."

As he said it, they heard more crashing sounds. The Troodons huddled together and Dacky shook his wings.

"Don't worry, I won't be long," replied Protos.

And to Marlin's surprise, he began looking through the books.

There were thousands of them, mostly old and dusty.

"Let me see now... *Lost Giants of the Triassic*...I enjoyed that one, especially chapter ten...*Creatures of the Arctic Forest*... very good but a bit chilly ...*The Great Cakes Cookery Book*, hmm...well that shouldn't be in here at all... Ah, here we are – *Secrets of the Jurassic Mountain*."

He looked up at them all and his eyes shone.

"It's a wonderful place, the Jurassic Mountain!"

He took hold of the book with his metal beak and pulled it. There was a scraping

sound and Marlin jumped backwards. The big wall map was moving!

It slid to one side. And behind it was a hidden passage sloping down into the dark.

Marlin peered inside and felt cool air on his face.

"Where does it go Protos?"

But before he could say any more Flame interrupted.

"Quick! They're here! The people are coming!"

Shouts echoed through the hall and then came the sound of heavy boots running towards them.

"Follow me now!" said Protos.

And he led them into the passage.

****

The wall map slid shut again – CLICK! – and then everything went black.

"Well that's a relief," the old creature said. "You know I wondered if it would still work…"

"But what now?" squawked Dacky.

One of the Troodons gave a frightened squeak.

"First things first," whispered Protos. "Are you there Steg? Can you give us some light?"

For a moment nothing happened, then Marlin saw the most magical sight.

The dark passage was filled with a sparkling light as the Stegosaurus began to glow. His towering armour plates were suddenly illuminated in gold and blue. The long spikes on his tail were shining bright red.

"Wow!" gasped the Troodons. "That's so cool!"

"Steg, that's brilliant!" exclaimed Marlin. "I didn't know you could do that!"

"It's a defensive trick," sniffed Steg. "Ancient stegosaurs probably did something similar."

"It's a good trick," beamed Protos. "And just the thing to help us now."

Then he lumbered forwards ahead of them into the gloom.

****

The passage wound downwards, twisting and turning. Down and down they went. It was long and narrow and they had to walk single file.

This was easy for Marlin, the Troodons and Dacky.

But the big Dinoteks had trouble. Steg's armour plates scraped along the passage roof. And coming behind the others, right at the back, Flame could only just squeeze himself through.

He closed his eyes and tried not to think about it too much. T-Rexs didn't like being closed in.

"Not far now," called Protos. "Keep going!"

And sure enough they soon came out into a wide, underground room. The walls were made with little bricks that looked very old. Marlin could see boxes and crates stretching away into the shadows.

"Here we are. Come in everyone," called Protos. "Welcome to the Underground Stores!"

Marlin watched the Dinoteks come crowding in. They gathered round in a group, all talking at once and telling Protos their news. The Troodons couldn't keep still, they were scampering around (and underneath) the big Dinoteks and they even started jumping across Steg's tail.

Marlin smiled. But it wasn't long before his smile faded.

Somewhere far above them he thought he heard rumbling sounds.

Chapter Eight

· · · · · · · · · · · · · · · ·

Gone!

The Demolition Army swarmed through the museum like angry ants. The bulldozer smashed its way into the entrance hall, destroying the glass door. And then dozens of black uniformed figures came scurrying in, clambering over the rubble and broken glass.

They found no dinosaurs.

Snickenbacker strode into the hall and Grubbler stomped in after him with a fierce grin on his face. He was looking forward to seeing the Dinoteks tied up in chains.

"Where are they?" he demanded.

"Hiding of course," said Snickenbacker.

Grubbler snorted angrily but

Snickenbacker laughed.

"Don't worry. We'll find them."

Then he turned to his people, and gave the order.

"Let's hunt!"

Immediately the black figures spread out and began moving through the halls. They would search all of the rooms one by one, pulling everything apart.

They had done this before and they were good at it.

The bulldozers rolled in too. They lowered their scoops and began shoving exhibits out of the way. They were making the path clear for the even bigger machines coming in behind.

"There may be some mess," smiled Snickenbacker as one of the glass cabinets was crunched up against the wall. "I'm afraid it can't be avoided."

Most museum managers would have cared about that. But Oliver Grubbler didn't. At that moment his mind was filled with only one thing.

"Just catch the dinosaurs!" he snarled.

And while everyone was rushing around, far above on the old stone walls, the carvings of animals looked down. There were creatures of all kinds, and delicate plants, curling and climbing upwards. This museum had been their home for over a hundred years – and they were only statues, not really alive.

But you could almost imagine them feeling sad at all the destruction below.

****

"I see...yes...Oh dear..."

Protos listened for a long time while Marlin and the Dinoteks told him about everything that had happened – about Grubbler and Snickenbacker, the Mayor and Inspector Bailey, the kind police detective.

Flame told him about Marlin's adventure in the Glass Tower.

"...biscuits, eh?! That was a good trick! I would never have thought of it..."

And when Marlin got to the part about the scrap metal plan Steg's armour plates bristled. That made the light in the room shimmer and all their shadows danced. Siggy squeaked and huddled next to Comp.

"Don't be frightened," Protos said to them. "We're all safe down here."

"But for how long?" said Steg. "We can't stay here forever. In the end we'll have to go out and fight."

Flame growled.

"Don't worry, we can beat them."

But Protos shook his head.

"Do you remember the Professor's Three Golden Rules?" he said gently.

They looked at each other and then Comp squeaked: "Where *is* the Professor? Will we see him soon?"

"Sshh!" said Flame. "Let Protos tell us the Three Golden Rules."

"One," said Protos. "We must always look after each other."

They all nodded.

"Two, we must never hurt anybody..."

They all shook their heads.

"And three, if somebody needs help we should always try to help them."

The Dinoteks nodded solemnly again.

Marlin could tell that they had all heard these rules before.

Then Protos sighed.

"And as for the Professor... I'm afraid we were all asleep for ages. Years in fact. I think the Professor must have died a long time ago."

The two little Troodons nodded – but they looked confused.

The older Dinoteks understood though and they hung their heads sadly.

"So now we're on our own," sighed Steg.

"No we're not! We have Marlin to help us now," said Protos. "He is very clever you know and brave too – although he *will* have to go home soon."

"Not before I've made sure you're all safe," said Marlin firmly.

Protos frowned but didn't reply.

He lumbered across the room into the shadows.

"There's something the Professor left for us..."

He reached down with his beak and picked something up. Then he laid it down at their feet. It was a long shape, bundled up in a cloth.

"Will you carry it, Flame? Very gently?"

"Yes," said the T-Rex solemnly.

He picked the bundle up, turned and laid it into the hatch on his back.

"Now let's just keep ourselves hidden underground for a bit longer," said Protos. "We can have a nice rest. Then as soon as it's dark outside it will be safe to leave."

The Dinoteks settled down and closed their eyes. And while they rested Marlin opened his rucksack. He took out the power charger and went round to all of them.

He attached the clips to each battery, just as Uncle Gus had said, and one at a time he powered them up.

He powered himself up too – in the rucksack he found a nice heap of sandwiches.

****

The sun was setting in front of the museum and the Demolition Army was fading into the shadows. As it grew darker

their strange black shapes became hard to see. And then, one by one, their headlights flicked on. They shone like eyes.

Grubbler was standing on the museum steps with his hands stuffed into his pockets. The Mayor was standing with him and for once he wasn't totally grey. There was a pink colour in his cheeks.

"The City Council will not be happy Grubbler," he tutted. "All this mess, all this damage. But there were no dinosaurs!"

The Mayor looked across at the flower beds, now trampled and churned. And he hadn't even seen the mess inside the museum yet!

"There were dinosaurs! I mean there *are* dinosaurs!" protested Grubbler. "They're just hiding…"

"He's right."

Snickenbacker came striding out, holding something in his hand.

"Look what we've found," he smiled. "There's a room full of old maps in there and my people discovered something very interesting."

The Mayor frowned.

"A map?"

"Not quite, but nearly," said Snickenbacker. "It's a plan. A plan of the museum."

He unfolded the paper.

"Now," he said, running his finger across

the old drawing. "It seems that this building has some secrets, Mr Grubbler."

"What do you mean?"

"There is a passage. It's shown on this plan but we can't find the door."

"A secret passage?" gasped the Mayor.

"Exactly," smiled Snickenbacker. "*That* is how the dinosaurs got away."

Grubbler clapped his hands together and his smile returned.

"So all we have to do is find the way in!"

He snatched the plan and spread it out on the ground. The Mayor knelt down beside him and they began to study it. But Snickenbacker laughed.

"We can be much cleverer than that," he said. "Don't look for the way in – look for the way out. That's where we'll catch them."

Chapter Nine

On the Run

"I think it's time to go," whispered Protos.

"Yes, I'm ready," said Marlin. He stood up and heaved the rucksack onto his back.

The Dinoteks shook themselves awake. Flame yawned and Dacky spread his wings, stretching across the whole room.

One of the little Troodons came over and sniffed at Marlin.

"Hello again Comp," Marlin smiled, patting its head.

The Troodon giggled.

"I'm Siggy," he squeaked, and ran off.

****

One by one they left the store room and headed along a tunnel. At the end was a door made of thick steel plates riveted together. It was rusty and Marlin guessed that it hadn't been opened for years. But it must have been well made because Protos pushed against it and it swung open with barely a creak.

They came out into a narrow cobbled street. It was already dark.

"Quietly now," whispered the Centrosaurus. "And Steg, you'd better turn off your lights."

Marlin looked both ways, up and down the street. There was a faint evening mist, making the street lights look soft and smudged. There was nobody in sight, nothing moving.

"We can't stay here," Marlin hissed.

Protos nodded.

"Yes, you're right," he said. "We must go north!"

Then he hesitated.

"Um, do you know which way north is?"

Marlin frowned and pointed up the road.

"I don't know – maybe that way?"

"Good!"

Protos heaved himself round.

"This way everyone, quickly."

And he lumbered along the road. The others followed him. Marlin carefully shut the metal door and ran after them.

They kept in the shadows close to the wall. There was a street lamp ahead, spreading a pool of light onto the road.

One after another they hurried under it —
their metal skins flashing as they passed —
then quickly got back into the dark.

Protos stopped. They had reached the
end of the street.

"Marlin you were right," he beamed. "We
came the right way. I remember this road!"

In front of them was a main road. It was
wide and brightly lit. As they stood there, a
line of cars sped by.

"But if we go out there we'll be
spotted!" Flame growled.

"We'll be quick," replied Protos. "We
must get across to the other side."

He pointed with his horn. Over the road
there was a dark gap between the buildings.

"You go first Flame. Go up that path.
Get to the very end and we'll all meet
there."

"OK."

The T-Rex looked up and down the road,
he sniffed the air — then leapt forwards and
was across in no more than three strides.
The Troodons scampered after him.

"Your turn Steg!"

Steg grumbled – he wasn't happy leaving the museum – but when he set off he was very quick. He dashed across the road and disappeared into the shadows after Flame.

More cars passed. They waited.

"Now us!" said Protos.

Dacky went first, flapping and hopping, with Marlin close after him.

Protos followed. He was slower than all the others – one of his back legs dragged when he tried to run – but he pushed on as fast as he could.

And he got to the other side not a moment too soon.

Protos was only just disappearing into the dark when a sinister black truck came speeding into the narrow street behind him.

****

Grubbler jumped out of the vehicle, still clutching the museum plan.

He looked up and down the road, then spotted the rusty door.

"There!"

He sprinted over to it and pressed his ear up against the cold metal.

"What are you doing?" asked Snickenbacker.

"Listening of course! It's an old hunter's trick. I'll be able to hear them before they come out. And then – "

But Snickenbacker chuckled.

"You're too late. They've already gone."

"Gone? How can you know that?!"

"Gone? How can you know that?!"

Snickenbacker pointed at the ground. At first Grubbler couldn't see anything, but then he noticed some rusty metal flakes scattered across the pavement.

"That door has just been opened," said Snickenbacker. "And look there."

He pointed along the road. There was a paving stone, cracked and slightly lifted. There were little fragments of stone and grit scattered around it that had not yet blown away. Something heavy had pressed on it, and cracked it, very recently.

Snickenbacker turned on his heels and walked back to the car. Grubbler hurried after him.

"So what do we do now?"

But Snickenbacker was already on his phone.

"Smith? We've found their trail. They're heading north. Get all the hunters moving. I want every road out of the city watched."

He snapped off the phone then turned back to Grubbler.

"They think they've got away but they've made a big mistake," he said. "They're in the open, they're too big to hide and they can't leave the city!"

****

Marlin followed Dacky up the path as it climbed uphill, winding between bushes and trees. It was quite wide – wide enough for a car to come along – but it was stony and full of pot-holes, not like a proper road. There were no street lights here and Marlin had to be careful not to trip.

"I can't see Protos yet," he said, looking over his shoulder.

"Don't worry boy, he'll come," cawed Dacky.

When he walked, the Pterosaur half hopped and half flapped. His wings brushed against the bushes.

"I'd rather be flying," he said. "But of course I don't want to leave you."

"It was good flying last night," said Marlin. "Thanks again for saving me!"

"Oh, don't mention it," said Dacky. "It was nothing, really…"

But in the dark Marlin could tell that the Pterosaur was pleased.

Marlin looked behind again.

"Dacky, do you think we should wait?"

"No, let's get to the top. Protos will find us."

They hurried on – but Marlin kept glancing backwards.

The path was becoming narrower and soon Dacky had to fold in his wings and walk without using them at all. That made him a lot slower.

Now, with trees all around them, it was much darker too.

Marlin stumbled.

But then Dacky stopped and whispered.

"Look ahead boy, there's a light!"

Marlin could see it, a faint glow shining red beneath the trees.

"It's Steg," he exclaimed. "He's lighting the way for us!"

****

In the street beside the museum Snickenbacker snapped off his phone and walked around to the back of his truck.

"What's happening now?" demanded Grubbler.

"My hunting squad is in position. Every route out of the city is blocked."

Snickenbacker swung open the car boot and leaned inside.

And when he stood up again Grubbler saw that he was holding some sort of weapon. It was long, like a rifle, but with two strange cylinders fixed to the barrel.

"Now comes the good part," said Snickenbacker. "Now we make our first catch!"

And he strode down the road, heading north, with Grubbler scurrying after him.

****

The Dinoteks were huddled together under a tree. They had followed the path as far as it would go and now the way ahead was tangled and overgrown.

"Where now?" hissed Steg. "This is a dead end, we'll have to turn back!"

Marlin stood anxiously looking behind. Then finally Protos lumbered into view.

"Well done," he puffed. "Is everyone here?"

"Yes, we're all here!" whispered Marlin.

The Centrosaurus glanced over his shoulder, back down the path. He seemed to be listening to something.

"I think we'd better move on," he said. "No time to rest. Flame, there should be a small path just through the bushes. It's quite steep, but not very long."

Flame nodded.

"I'll find it."

And Marlin heard the undergrowth cracking and crunching as the T-Rex pushed through it.

"Follow behind Flame everyone."

They moved forwards in a line and Steg kept a faint light glowing to help show the way. Marlin walked beside Protos again.

"But where are we going?" he whispered.

"To a safe place I hope, Marlin," replied the old creature. "I came up here many years ago. The Professor showed me. I just hope I've remembered it correctly."

He glanced backwards again, listening.

"We need to be quick, I think..."

But before he could explain there was

a crashing sound in the bushes ahead and Flame re-appeared.

"Protos! We can't go this way!" he hissed.

"Why not? What's wrong Flame?" demanded Steg.

"There's a creature!" exclaimed the T-Rex. "A gigantic metal snake!"

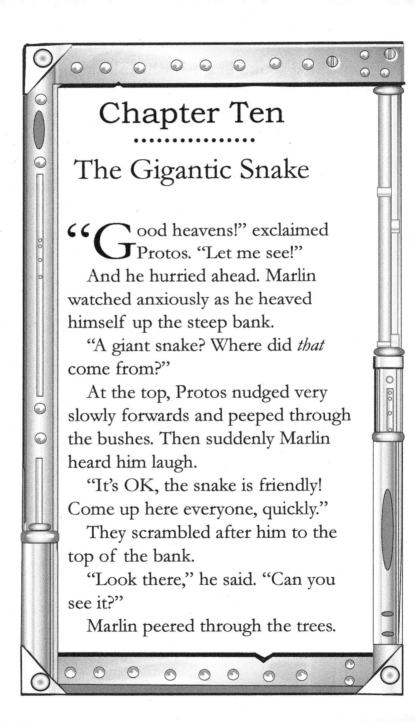

Chapter Ten

· · · · · · · · · · · · · ·

The Gigantic Snake

"Good heavens!" exclaimed Protos. "Let me see!"

And he hurried ahead. Marlin watched anxiously as he heaved himself up the steep bank.

"A giant snake? Where did *that* come from?"

At the top, Protos nudged very slowly forwards and peeped through the bushes. Then suddenly Marlin heard him laugh.

"It's OK, the snake is friendly! Come up here everyone, quickly."

They scrambled after him to the top of the bank.

"Look there," he said. "Can you see it?"

Marlin peered through the trees.

There was an open space and in the moonlight he could see the creature that Flame had spotted.

It was lying there with its long black body, totally still. Waiting in ambush? It stretched away into the distance. It really was huge...

But suddenly Marlin laughed too.

"It's not a snake!"

"What is it then?" frowned Flame.

"A train!"

Protos led them all forwards.

"Oh, yes of course," muttered Flame, embarrassed. "I should have thought of that."

"What's a train?" hissed Steg.

The Troodons shook their heads. They didn't know either.

"We could ask Professor Marlin," squeaked Comp.

"He's not a Professor," snorted Steg.

Then they followed after the others.

****

The Dinoteks gathered together by the railway track and stared up at the goods train parked in front of them.

It was long, with high, closed wagons at the front and a line of open, flat carriages at the back.

It wasn't moving, but Marlin could hear the whir and click of its motors. He looked down the line and saw a red light.

A red signal.

That's why the train had stopped.

"It will go as soon as the light turns green," he whispered.

"Yes," nodded Protos. "I think we're just in time. We must all get on board."

"I can't get up there," protested Steg.

But Protos was looking behind again,

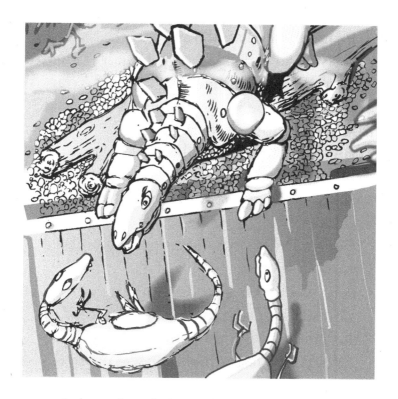

peering anxiously into the dark.

"Hmmm…I think we should be quick,"
he said.

Straight away the two Troodons hopped
up onto the nearest wagon.

"Come on Steg! It's easy!" squeaked
Siggy.

Dacky flapped his wings twice, and was
up beside them.

Protos looked at Marlin.

"Now you've helped us I think it's time for you to be getting home," he began. "Your teacher won't be happy if you are too tired for school and also there's a – "

But Marlin shook his head.

"I'm coming all the way!" he said firmly. "And don't worry about school, it's the holidays."

Before Protos could argue he scrambled up onto the train.

Steg was still hesitating

"I'll never get up there," he grumbled. "And neither will you Protos!"

"Yes you will. Both of you," grunted Flame.

He was dragging something towards them in his jaws – a massive fallen tree trunk. He dropped it right next to the track.

"Up you go Steg!"

The armoured creature snorted impatiently – but he clambered up on to the trunk and began balancing along it. At last he got his front feet onto the edge of the wagon and gave a mighty heave. He was up!

"Well done!" cawed Dacky.

"Cool!" squeaked the Troodons.

Steg bristled.

"It wasn't hard."

Now Flame dragged the tree trunk along to the next wagon.

"Your turn Protos!"

"Thank you," said the old creature.

He copied Steg, balancing in the same way, and got his front feet onto the wagon. But suddenly Marlin shouted a warning.

"The signal! It's green!"

****

There was a heavy clunk and the train started to move.

Protos didn't have the strength for the jump. He clung onto the wagon, but his back legs slipped off the tree trunk and dragged along in the gravel.

He couldn't hold on!

Just before he fell, he had time to call out one last thing.

"Look after each other...find somewhere

to hide… I'll come to you!"

The train lurched forwards.

The wheels turned faster, faster.

Protos fell – but then suddenly he felt himself rising again. He was actually floating up onto the wagon! He looked down and realised that Flame was pushing him up with his powerful head. There was a grinding of metal and the T-Rex groaned with the great effort of lifting such a weight.

"That's it! Come on! Come on!" he grunted.

And suddenly Protos was safely on board. Flame had done it!

Protos turned to say thank you – but even at that moment Flame himself stumbled.

His claws slipped in the gravel and he crashed over.

"Flame!" shouted Marlin – and the others called out too.

They watched in horror as the great Dinotek struggled to stand while the train gathered speed and rattled away into the night.

Chapter Eleven

·············

Flame Alone

Flame stood up again and shook himself. He turned to see the train disappearing. And then two men stepped out in front of him.

The big one he recognised. He was the man who had been standing in front of the museum all day. The man

who had shouted into the megaphone.

The T-Rex sniffed at him. He knew the scent. It was Oliver Grubbler, their enemy.

The other man – the thin one – stepped forwards.

He lifted something, and smiled. There was a sound – BANG! – and something shot through the air.

Flame looked down, puzzled. A net was tangled around his legs.

BANG!

Now there was another net. It was covering his head. He shook it, but it wouldn't come off. That made the men laugh.

The big one, Grubbler, pointed at him.

"Not so scary now are you T-Rex?!"

Then he turned to his friend.

"Can I have a go?"

"Be my guest!"

BANG! BANG!

More nets. Flame was becoming tangled!

Grubbler raised the gun above his head and shouted.

"I am Grubbler the Beast-Slayer!"

Then he fired three more shots and the
nets began to wrap more tightly.

Flame looked at Grubbler.

Then he raised his head – stretched his
jaws – and snapped the
nets.

He straightened
his legs and stepped
forwards. More of the

nets snapped. Finally, he shook himself and
they all fell away, landing in a heap at his feet.

Both men stared at him, open mouthed,
too astonished to even move.

Flame stared back at them.

The Second Golden Rule, we must never hurt

anybody…

He turned and sprinted along the track.

****

How fast could an ancient T-Rex have run? Experts are still not sure.

But there's no doubt about Flame. He was fast, very fast.

If you'd been alive in the Cretaceous era you might have been lucky enough to see something as good as this – or even *half* as good!

Flame came powering along the line faster than any creature in history.

He pounded forwards and the train came into view. He could see his friends. Now they were cheering for him, calling out his name.

He ran faster, head low, tail thrashing from side to side.

But the train was getting faster too.

It came around the bend – rattling and hissing – and onto the straight track. Then it began to pick up serious speed. Flame knew that it would soon accelerate beyond even his pace.

But he fixed his eyes ahead and pushed harder – *harder!* – he was *not* going to be left behind.

There was a moment when time seemed to stand still.

At that moment Flame and the train were going at exactly the same speed. A second later, and time would move on again, and then the train would pull away from him.

But just before that happened Flame threw himself forwards.

CRASH!

He landed on the last flat carriage.

It felt as though the wagon might be knocked off its rails. But it wasn't and Flame sat up, grinning.

"Do I need a ticket?"

Chapter Twelve

· · · · · · · · · · · · · · ·

Follow the Dinosaurs!

Snickenbacker walked across to the broken nets. He reached down for one, held it up in his thin hands and looked closely at the ripped ends.

And to Grubbler's surprise he was smiling.

"Excellent!" he exclaimed.

"What do you mean?!" spluttered Grubbler. "They got away again and your net-gun didn't work!"

"My net-gun didn't work," replied Snickenbacker, taking his friend by the arm. "But I have other weapons that are much better. Wait till you see them Grubbler! And now at last I have found something worth hunting!"

He led Grubbler away from the railway line and they scrambled back down the steep path.

Snickenbacker pulled out his phone.

"Smith? Yes it's me. There's a railway line north of the museum. A train just left from here and the dinosaurs are on it. Find out where it's going!"

****

At the police headquarters, very close to the museum, Inspector Bailey was thinking about dinosaurs too.

Ever since her encounter with Grubbler yesterday, and her talk with Marlin, she'd been puzzling over it.

She had liked Marlin. The museum manager had called him a thief and that clearly wasn't true. But the boy's story had been very odd.

Dinoteks — machines coming to life — it couldn't really be true could it?

There was a knock on her door. A visitor...

The door opened and a man stepped in.

Almost without thinking about it Inspector Bailey noticed everything about his appearance – it was the habit of a police detective. He was in his sixties, early sixties probably. He had wild grey hair, dark eyes and a moustache.

He also had rough hands – so he was a builder maybe, or a mechanic?

Oil around the fingernails, a mechanic then…

He had a kind face.

"Please sit down. How can I help you?"

"Inspector, I need to find the dinosaurs."

"Well," she smiled. "You're not the only one. Today, everybody seems to be looking for them."

"Are you?"

"Actually no. It's not a police matter. No crime has been committed. And I'm not even convinced that these creatures exist – Mr?"

"Gus. They do exist. My nephew Marlin is with them."

Now Inspector Bailey was interested. She leaned forwards.

"Marlin Maxton? The boy who said he

could bring them to life?"

Him again...

"Yes, that's him, he's a great lad. He's helping the creatures. And they're called Dinoteks – they're not dangerous Inspector Bailey. They are perfectly safe."

"And you say Marlin is with them now Mr Gus? Is that wise?"

The old man scratched his head.

"I can't tell you why exactly. But I know the Dinoteks are good. They will look after Marlin, Inspector, I'm certain about that. And he'll look after them."

Inspector Bailey studied the man's face.

He was rather eccentric looking but he was honest.

"Well I'm glad you came to see me Mr Gus. Perhaps it is time the police got involved with this case..."

Yes, she thought, it was time she asked a few questions. All that disturbance at the museum...all those people running about in black uniforms! Something about this business wasn't right.

She didn't trust Oliver Grubbler –

and she definitely didn't like Howard Snickenbacker.

"Thank you for coming to see me Mr Gus. I'm going to investigate. I'll see what I can find out…"

She stood up.

"Do you know where the Dinoteks are now?"

"No. But I think they've got away somehow."

She sighed.

"Well, I only hope they've gone somewhere safe."

****

"Excellent! Get everyone there at once Smith – and make sure they're ready!"

Snickenbacker snapped off his phone and smiled at Grubbler.

"We've got them!"

"What do you mean?"

"In exactly one hour and twenty three minutes the train will be arriving at its last and only stop. When it does, my people will be there waiting."

Grubbler grinned.

"Now, shall we go back to my headquarters?" said Snickenbacker. "You can look at my Special Weapons while we wait for the good news!"

Chapter Thirteen

· · · · · · · · · · · · · · ·

The Strange Star

The train was racing through the night at full speed and Marlin was huddled close to Protos, sheltering from the wind. He had his heavy coat pulled tightly around him.

The city was now far behind and so were their enemies. They had escaped.

But Protos looked worried.

"We have to get off," he frowned.

"What's wrong?"

"If we stay on this train we'll go too far. We need to go north, then west a bit."

Protos thought for a moment. Then he looked across at Dacky who was crouching on the next wagon, sheltering behind Steg.

"Dacky," he called. "Is it true? Can you really fly?"

****

Two minutes later Dacky was standing on the edge of the wagon, gripping it tight with his claws. He looked straight ahead, into the rushing wind. This could be dangerous...

His wings might be ripped off by the force of the air. Or he might lose control of his flight and crash to the ground.

He closed his eyes and counted to three.

Then he went.

WOOOOSH!

The speed of the train shot him upwards.

He felt his wings tug and strain. But he didn't crash... he soared!

It must have been like this millions of years ago when the great reptiles launched themselves from cliff tops above stormy oceans.

AAAAK! AAAAK!

He cried out in triumph and then had an urge to soar upwards, to fly higher and

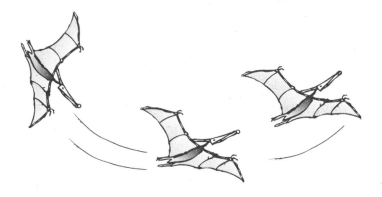

faster.

But he didn't. He flicked his wings round and wheeled away along the track, overtaking the train. Far below, his friends cheered him on. All except Steg who was watching grim faced.

In Dacky's beak was one of Steg's beautiful red tail lights.

Steg could see it winking in the sky like a strange star, getting smaller and smaller.

Protos' plan was simple. Dacky would fly ahead and leave the light by the side of the track. The train driver would think it was a signal to stop.

"Everybody, get ready to jump!" Protos called out above the roar of the wind.

Marlin came to stand next to him.

He looked at the ground rushing past.

"I hope Dacky can do it," he said.

Soon Dacky had got far enough ahead. He swooped low and spotted a good place. A tree with branches hanging close to the line. It was perfect, exactly the right height for a railway signal.

He landed smoothly and tucked Steg's light between two branches, then flapped off to hide in the undergrowth.

He had just got out of sight when the train came racing into view.

But sure enough the driver spotted the light and slammed on the brakes.

SCREEEEECH!

In the darkness the Dinoteks jumped and clambered down – Protos landed heavily, but quickly followed the others into the trees.

They kept very still in the dark for what seemed like ages.

Nothing moved.

Then at last the train hissed, clunked and moved forwards again, faster and faster until it was gone.

Dacky flew down and they rushed over to him.

"Well done! Brilliant flying!"

But Dacky wasn't smiling.

He hopped over to Steg.

"I'm sorry," he said. "I couldn't save your light. The train driver took it."

Steg sighed.

"It doesn't matter," he said. "At least we're all safe."

******

They walked away from the railway line. Steg went in front and lit up his armour to show them the way.

But now his tail only had three lights, not four.

"We'll get you another one," promised Protos. "It will be the best we can find."

"And I'll fit it for you," said Marlin.

"It's OK. I'm not worried," shrugged Steg. He was trying to sound cheerful.

They walked on, looking for somewhere to rest, and Protos told them all a story.

He talked about where they would be going. There were fossils in the ground there, layers and layers of them waiting to be discovered, some from creatures quite unknown. And he talked about all the things living in the woods — birds, mammals, insects, plants — and all the secret places there were to explore.

And then he stopped.

"Now it's time to sleep," he said.

The huddled together under a wide tree. The Troodons sheltered next to Steg. Dacky flapped up into one of the branches. Marlin curled up on the ground beside Flame and felt the warmth of his motor as it purred deep inside. And Protos settled down at the edge of the circle, looking out into the night.

****

Snickenbacker and Grubbler were having dinner when, at exactly midnight, the phone rang. It was Smith.

"No! That's impossible!"

For once Snickenbacker was not calm.

He screwed up his fist and thumped the dining table so hard that the plates rattled.

"What is it? What's wrong?" exclaimed Grubbler.

"They escaped – again!" hissed Snickenbacker. "But how?"

He stood up and began pacing around the room.

"It's impossible. They were on that train…"

Then he walked across to his desk and sat down.

Grubbler watched him.

All at once, Snickenbacker's face didn't look angry any more — he smiled coldly and picked up his phone again.

"Smith? It's time. First thing tomorrow morning — wake up the *Raptor*…"

Chapter Fourteen

········

Little Dragon

Marlin woke first and found all the Dinoteks asleep. All except for Protos. It was a grey, damp morning and the old creature was staring into the distance. There were trees all around them and far away hills with their tops hidden in mist.

"Hello Marlin! Did you get some rest?"

"Yes," Marlin yawned. "Did you?"

Protos shook his head.

"No! This time I stayed awake all night. I've spent too many years sleeping. Did you know the stars move across the sky?"

Marlin shook his head.

"They do if you watch them for long enough," said Protos. "They go circling overhead."

"And where are *we* going?" said a voice. It was Steg, now awake too.

"Somewhere safe," said Protos – but he wouldn't say any more about it, not until everyone was awake.

Marlin rummaged in his rucksack and grinned. Uncle Gus had packed breakfast for him too. It was almost as if he'd known that Marlin would be travelling!

He unwrapped the paper and found a chunky cheese sandwich inside. And there was a bottle of water.

I wonder what he's doing now? I hope he's not worried...

"Do you have a phone?" asked Protos suddenly, as if he'd guessed Marlin's thoughts.

Marlin shook his head.

"Hmm…" nodded the old creature, almost talking to himself. "We must find a phone…"

Then Protos bowed his head and seemed to close his eyes. One by one the Dinoteks woke up. Comp and Siggy began

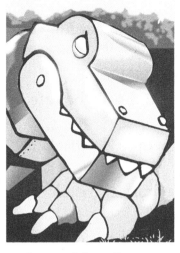

scampering around between the trees. Dacky hopped down from his branch and Flame stretched and yawned.

Protos didn't move. Marlin watched him. He seemed to be waiting for something.

Finally, the sun came out and the old creature looked up. He heaved himself round to face them all.

"We can go now!" he said. "We've got a long way to walk today but I'm sure you'll all like it where we're going."

"But where *are* we going?" asked Marlin.

Protos looked at Flame.

"Do you have it? The thing I gave you?"

"Yes."

Flame turned his head and lifted the

217

bundle from his back. He laid it carefully on the ground.

"There is a place called the Jurassic Mountain," said Protos. "And we'll be safe there."

"What about the bad people?" squeaked Comp.

"They won't be able to hurt us," said Protos. "Because of this…"

Protos unwrapped the bundle and pulled out a sheet of paper.

"This is very precious. The Professor left it for us."

"What is it?" cawed Dacky.

"It's called a Legal Document."

The Dinoteks gathered round and looked at it.

"It's just paper," frowned Steg. "With funny lines…"

"Words. Writing. It says the mountain belongs to us."

"A whole mountain?" exclaimed Marlin.

"Yes."

Protos picked up the paper and carefully handed it to Marlin.

"Will you look after this for us?"

Marlin nodded, and he opened his rucksack. There was a pocket inside and he slipped the paper into it.

"So where is it then?" asked Steg. "Where *is* the mountain?"

Protos shook his head.

"I don't know the way from here…"

Steg snorted.

"But there is someone who can help us," continued Protos.

He reached down and pulled at the cloth again. Something rolled out and everyone gasped.

****

There, lying on the ground, was an enormous dragonfly. It had a long, thin body – only just smaller than the Troodons – and four slender wings, neatly folded.

"Another Dinotek!" cheered Marlin.

"Yes," smiled Protos.

"He's cute!" squeaked Siggy. "So tiny!"

"Can he fly?" cawed Dacky.

"Yes," said Protos. "He's a Meganeura and his name is Little Dragon."

Marlin delved into his rucksack again.

"I can charge his battery!"

"No need," said Protos. "Look. He's powered by the sun!"

And sure enough, as they watched the little creature began to move. Its wings flickered and twitched and then they spread open.

It lay still for a moment longer, taking in the heat, then suddenly its wings buzzed and it flew up into the air.

"Hello Little Dragon," laughed Protos. "Do you know where we are?"

The creature buzzed around, flitting away through the trees, then it came back and perched on Protos' horn.

"We're lost! Can you show us the way to the mountain?"

The Meganeura took off again and flew away.

"Quickly now," said Protos. "Follow after him everyone!"

They all set off, striding, running, clunking and scampering – chasing through the trees – and it was such fun that even Steg couldn't help laughing.

The only one who didn't run was Dacky.

He wouldn't stay on the ground now! He spread his great wings and took to the air.

****

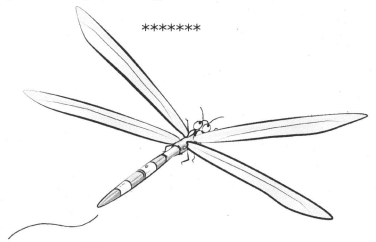

A nd at that very moment, far away in the south, the *Raptor* was taking to the air too.

It was Howard Snickenbacker's favourite machine – his hunting helicopter.

Its sharp rotor-blades spun faster and faster, chopping at the air. Then it left the ground.

It picked up speed. It soared over the city and headed north, following the railway line.

The end
(for now)
The Dinoteks have
narrowly escaped –
now you can read
their next
thrilling
adventures
in book #3:
*The Secret Dinosaur
Jurassic Adventure*

About the author

N.S.Blackman has been writing and illustrating dinosaur stories since his early school days in the Cretaceous period.

His current habitat is London where he lives not far from Crystal Palace (where the world's oldest life-size dinosaur models also have their home).

If you have any questions about the Dinoteks or would like to send in your own designs and pictures to N.S.Blackman visit www.dinoteks.com

Find Dinotek colouring sheets and more at dinoteks.com

Discover more of Marlin's thrilling dinosaur adventures at www.dinoteks.com